Darkness Descends

Prequel to Chronicle of Ceres

CL LaVigne

Cover Designed by MiblArt

Darkness Descends

(Prequel, Chronicle of Ceres) - 1st Edition

www.cllavigne.com

www.facebook.com/CLLaVigneAuthor

ISBN (eBook): 979-8-9884845-5-4

ISBN (paperback): 979-8-9884845-6-1

Contents

Introduction

Darkness Descends is the prequel to the magical-realism books of Chronicle of Ceres.

One thousand years ago, our planet flourished in peace and prosperity. Natural magic sustained the world with an endless supply of positive energy.

There was no famine, no poverty, and no hatred.

Then evil arrived on Earth.

This novella explores how the Yfel Brethren came into existence, why The Cererian Prophecy was created, and how four magicians and one shaman would be chosen to save the world.

To eradicate evil, there must be sacrifices.

Chapter 1

Unbearable Bodies

A FAMILY OF RAVENS circled the valley, riding the thermals and searching for death.

Stygian shielded his eyes and squinted into the sun. "This cursed star has followed me for seven days," he growled. "When will the cold, dark night return?"

He and his soldiers bunched together on the banks of a small creek meandering through an immense wildflower meadow. The sun's rays glinted off the gurgling stream—a shimmering silver thread stitched into a fragrant, floral landscape.

"We have arrived in the season of summer, Commander." Stygian glared at the soldier who spoke. The small man recoiled from his leader's gaze. Fear paralyzed him, his lips rounded for the next word he intended to speak.

"And?" demanded Stygian. "Speak, Andee, speak!"

Trembling, the soldier stuttered, "The sun...never...uh...sets...in...this...region." He hung his head, fearing retribution from his commander, expecting the beating that had been meted on all of them since their arrival on Earth seven days earlier.

Stygian sneered and turned away. Closing his eyes, he mumbled a curse. His lips stretched thin from concentration, and his fists clenched in front of his body as the conjuring continued. The long, pointed nail on each thumb stabbed into his palms. Droplets of blood streamed onto the ground, turning the yellow sand into a dark mahogany. The soldiers shifted uneasily, their gazes darting nervously to each other. Their leader acted irrationally, and his unpredictable temper grew more volatile every day.

In a telepathic chorus, they called out to their comrade: *Darrius, can you intervene?*

Darrius stood to the side, observing his friend. Blood magic was only used in extreme situations, and Stygian's actions deeply concerned him.

"Stygian, may I have a word?" Darrius did not address his friend as Commander or Leader. Both men were of equal status and arrived with a shared leadership of the exploration team. But almost immediately upon landing a week earlier, Stygian's nature began changing. His angry outbursts were commonplace and quickly escalated to vicious beatings for even the most minor infractions. Oftentimes, following a stream of volatile rants Stygian would retreat to his tent for a period of moody isolation.

No longer satisfied with sharing leadership with Darrius, Stygian announced himself to be the commander of their small band of soldiers. Darrius hadn't pressed the issue at the time. He had no desire to lead, and his friend's abilities and experience as a shrewd warrior were well-respected on Ceres. But now, with Stygian's unpredictable nature and the fear exhibited by the soldiers, Darrius doubted his decision to relinquish full control to his friend.

"Darrius, do not bother me," Stygian cautioned through gritted teeth. A steady stream of blood dripped from his hands forming a dark pool of viscous fluid that spread along the ground.

"Stygian, blood magic is a Cererian ritual. Attempting to perform it in your human form is futile since you won't be able to discharge the negative energy from your body. You'll only be successful in losing blood that your body needs to remain alive." Stygian's shoulders shuddered. It was a slight movement, but Darrius saw an opening, a sign that his friend was listening. Encouraged, Darrius tried a different tactic—appealing to Stygian's ego. "Our group cannot carry forth on our mission without our leader. I implore you to stop...now."

Stygian dropped his hands. Gashes in both palms angrily flared, blood flowed freely onto the ground. He had successfully punctured a hole through each palm, leaving a small exit wound on the back of each hand. He turned toward Darrius.

"Perhaps you're right. I wouldn't want to leave you all alone in this hostile place." A forced smile flitted across his face as he gazed upward at the sun. "That cursed ball of light infuriates me! I wish I could knock it out of the sky with my thoughts!" He touched his forehead and narrowed his gaze at the sun for several moments. "Alas, I can't even do that."

The men studied each other, probing each other's minds. Darrius sensed anger and disappointment simmering deep within his friend. Stygian smirked, feeling only calm and patience from Darrius. "Darrius, does nothing upset you?"

Darrius gathered Stygian's hands and lifted them to his mouth to perform a healing ritual. "You are so predictable," Stygian sniped. "You have always been the caring one." Despite the tone in his words, Stygian didn't resist Darrius' offer. Stygian's pupils enlarged, eager to have the healing magic penetrate his skin. This form of energy dove deep into the soul, igniting a fire that coursed through the veins. It pricked the primal areas of Cererian existence and caused incredible pain or pleasure depending on the needs of the recipient.

Carefully cradling his friend's injured hands, Darrius parted his lips and gently blew. A cooling breath carrying Cererian healing power, brushed over the wounds. Stygian closed his eyes and moaned. After a minute, his eyes flashed open—brilliant emerald, green with specks of fluorescent gold—and he yanked his hands away from Darrius. "Enough, Darrius. I can bear no more."

Darrius gazed at his friend. In this body, Stygian was a stranger, a humanoid imposter, residing in that form for one purpose: to explore the planet, collect data, and establish contact with the inhabitants. The being he's known for over a thousand years existed deep inside this human shell, but Stygian was changing. His demeanor was growing darker each passing day.

Darrius mulled over the possibilities: *Did we miscalculate the effects of this planet's energy on our human bodies? Are Stygian's emotional outbursts the unresolved feelings that were buried along with the human host body from where the Harvesters obtained the DNA?*

Like his friend, Darrius possessed the common Cererian trait of intense green eyes. Both men stood over six foot tall and possessed the youthful skin of men in their twenties. But the similarities ended there. Their human bodies were vastly different, like night and day.

Darrius' smooth mocha skin, black curly hair, and strong jaw-line contrasted to Stygian's pale complexion, flaxen hair, and delicate features. The DNA for Darrius was found in the southwest region of the British Isles. Stygian's body was born of a Nordic warrior found buried deep beneath a glacier just beyond the petrified pillars of a long-forgotten village.

But these dissimilar physical traits were by design. Each soldier in the expedition carried unique DNA, a careful consideration of the Harvesters who visited Earth decades earlier. Their plan was simple: locate deceased, human donors who represented a diverse cross-section of the world's population and then reanimate bodies from their harvested DNA.

Harvesters extracted small amounts of genetic material from cadavers using magical transference by hovering their hands over the body. The rising molecules were captured and immediately shuttled back to Ceres via a portal to the dwarf planet. The first volunteers—Cererian soldiers—fused their energetic lifeforce with the human genetic material. This process involved merging the DNA molecules into the energy cells of the Cererian candidate. Over five days, the volunteers slowly transformed into physical duplicates of their hosts.

Darrius had encouraged Stygian to join him for the inaugural mission to Earth. They'd been on many explorations throughout the galaxy but had never been to the blue planet. *I know you can't resist a good adventure, Stygian, even if it means shedding your Cererian body for that of an alien.* Convincing his friend was easy.

Stygian cocked his head. "Alien...you think of us as aliens?" Lost in his musings, Darrius gazed at his friend through unfocused eyes. "Darrius, did you hear me?"

Abruptly, Darrius' pupils enlarged as his eyes refocused. His face flushed. A warm smile could not conceal his embarrassment. "You caught me daydreaming. When I look at you, I'm fascinated by all the angles and curves of your human body. Very different from our oval Cererian bodies of pure energy."

Stygian winced. He wasn't one for pleasantries and Darrius' remarks made him uncomfortable. He abruptly changed the subject. "It would appear that your healing magic worked." He lifted his hands and flipped them over. His pale skin bore no marks, not even a scar. Darrius nodded, pleased with the results.

Stygian whirled to rejoin his men, but Darrius clamped a hand on his shoulder stopping him. "Stygian?"

Like a rabid dog, Stygian rushed toward Darrius, his lips curled back from his teeth. "How dare you detain me! Remember your place!"

Confusion fluttered across Darrius' face as he withdrew his hand. Surrendering to his friend's fury, Darrius held his palms up. He needed to disarm the situation before it escalated. "My apologies, Stygian. I meant no disrespect." Darrius dipped his head, a Cererian gesture of respect.

Like a bull poised to charge, Stygian furiously panted, his nostrils flaring. He glared at Darrius through bulging, bloodshot eyes. His fists tightened and the muscles across his face twitched as thoughts of destruction raced through his mind.

Darrius remained calm. He removed all emotion from his face—his eyes drooped, and his mouth relaxed. Despite his height, he tried to appear smaller and non-threatening by rolling his shoulders down and forward. A sense of calm eked from his pores as he breathed evenly, discreetly blowing healing energy toward his friend. It was risky. Stygian could notice his efforts and retaliate, but Darrius had to try.

Several tense seconds passed before Stygian's eyes relaxed, slowly opening and closing like a sleepy child. He yawned, releasing the rigid muscles gripping his sneer. Finally, his arms fell by his side, fingers uncurling. Darrius continued the healing magic until Stygian's breaths appeared slow and steady, and his head dipped toward his chest.

"Stygian?" Darrius whispered.

"I feel strange," his friend squeaked in a strangled whisper. "I no longer feel as though I can control this body." Anguish colored his reply. Stygian raised his head. His eyes blurred with tears. Puzzled, he dabbed at them and studied the moisture. "This is new," he said as he pushed a finger toward Darrius.

Darrius nodded. "Emotion. Your situation pains you and your body responded to your torment."

"It's a weakness." Stygian sighed a heavy breath. "You had a question?"

Moments earlier, Stygian was on the verge of attacking him. But now, his friend appeared calm and receptive. Darrius glanced at the soldiers who impatiently shuffled their feet, anxiously watching the interaction between the two friends. He approached Stygian and leaned close so he could whisper, "What did you hope to achieve with the blood magic?"

Stygian's demeanor changed. The emotional calm provided by the healing magic vanished releasing the tortured soul that resided deep inside Stygian. "That's what I like about you, Darrius. You're blunt and don't waste my time with weak words." A forced smile flashed across Stygian's face and then disappeared.

The two men studied each other for several tense moments before Stygian mentally replied, *I do not care to share my reasons with these soldiers. What I do and what I feel are none of their business.* Stygian reached forward with his needle-sharp thumbnail and lightly touched Darrius' cheek. A small slit appeared, blood droplets popping along the seam. Despite the searing pain, Darrius did not flinch. Stygian's lips curled upward in a wicked sneer, relishing the power he exhibited over his friend. *I hoped to transform my body back to my Cererian form. This human body is unbearable. The emotions and the physical limitations annoy me.*

Darrius listened attentively. He looked beyond Stygian and scanned the soldiers' faces. They were glazed with a mixture of dread and concern. *But you cannot undo that which has been done. We were given these forms so that we could successfully interact with the natural populations. We cannot abandon these vessels that sustain our lives.*

"I will not accept this fate!"

Stygian's bellow startled the soldiers. Their eyes widened in fright. Andee cowered behind his son, Benedict, while Thane and Everild stumbled backward, concerned that Stygian's anger would engulf them like a fiery tsunami. In the moment of his tantrum, the tall man with flaxen hair and sunburned, skin appeared more like an unruly child and not the Nordic warrior whose DNA was used to reanimate his human body.

Cererian outbursts were rare. The beings from the dwarf planet over two hundred million miles from Earth had evolved, shedding physical bodies for forms consisting primarily of pure energy—transparent, egg-shaped forms bearing two slender appendages on either side, and two dark circles near the top. Tangible

logic motivated them, not emotions, which were deemed unnec-
essary.

Andee discreetly peered at his son, Benedict, and mentally messaged, *Stygian grows angrier each day. Our leader's behavior is
troubling.*

Benedict gazed at Stygian who had retreated to the shade of a
nearby sugar pine tree. The young man did not resemble Andee at
all. He stretched almost seven feet tall with gangly arms and legs
that sprouted from his lean body as if he was made of rubber. His
grayish-white skin gave him the appearance of a cadaver, sprouting
long, white hair.

*It's the land, father. The unusual energy is affecting our minds. I
feel it too.*

"Thane. Everild. Come here!" Stygian glared at his men, jerking his
hand impatiently.

The two soldiers ran to his side and replied in unison, "Sir!"

A sneer knifed across Stygian's face which flamed red from the
sun's heat. He narrowed his eyes and wrinkled his nose in deep
disgust as if smelling something unpleasant. The soldiers lowered
their eyes and clenched their hands, fearing punishment, which
had become progressively brutal since their arrival on Earth.

Stygian stared at their bowed heads. For a flicker of a second, he
considered bashing in their skulls. But a slight movement caught
his eye. The hands of his soldiers trembled. Stygian's mouth jerked
upward into a twisted grin. He breathed deeply, inhaling the lus-

cious scent of intense fear. A shadow of superiority scurried across his face. Through fear his men would do his bidding no matter what he asked.

"We have been walking for seven days, and we have yet to encounter any life forms. How do you explain this?"

Thane and Everild exchanged sideways glances. The men panted from the heat and the terror raced upward from the pits of their stomachs. They didn't have an answer, but their leader expected a reply. They mutely responded with shrugs.

Stygian tilted his head back and screamed into the sky. "Where are the humans?"

His words raced across the valley before reaching Denali's peak. The earth spirit captured his words and swallowed them, silencing the echo. An eerie quietness drifted across the landscape. The soldiers peered into the distance while Stygian tilted his head, listening for words that would never return. Darrius' intuition nagged him. Something was amiss, beyond the bizarre actions of his comrade.

Nearby, a family of ravens observed the humans. Having settled onto a sandbar several yards down the creek, the corvids had been pecking the water for crabs and minnows when Stygian's wail interrupted their hunt. The matriarch shifted her gaze from Stygian to Denali. Unspoken words flowed between them. After several moments, the raven squawked, and the flock launched into the sky.

Sweat rolled down his cheeks and frothy spittle flew from his mouth as Stygian paced back and forth. He released his fury on the soldiers, screaming at the defeated men. Occasionally he stopped and threatened one of the soldiers with a balled fist, shaking it in their face, demanding an explanation. But there were no answers.

The terrified men remained at attention, trembling, as their commander showered them with insults.

Veins in his neck bulged like thick cords. Adrenalin surged through Stygian's body. His nostrils flared, tantalized by the stress hormones secreted by the soldiers' bodies. He inhaled greedily, latching on to the exhilaration each breath delivered. Like a parched man clutching a cup of cool water, Stygian eagerly drank in the fear-filled emotions. Consuming the misery of others fueled his arrogance and suppressed his own emotions, feelings that he deemed weaknesses.

Darrius sighed. This was not the Stygian he knew. It pained him to watch his friend transform into a despicable leader. The person antagonizing the soldiers was not his trusted friend. Within the first seven days of their arrival on Earth to study the inhabitants, the soldiers had collected more data on their own physical and mental failures than on the biological offerings of the planet. A troubled smile flickered across his face. The irony was amusing. But there was nothing funny about their situation. What toll were these mood swings having on his friend and the mission?

Darkness descends. The melodic voice floated in his mind like the tinkling of a small bell.

Darrius held his breath. It wasn't Stygian or the soldiers. He surveyed the landscape, looking for anything out of place. A black cloud of ravens flew overhead. An unsettling stillness thickened the air.

A gentle thrumming began. Initially, the hum was low, almost inaudible. Then it grew in tempo until the ground vibrated beneath his feet and the wildflowers quavered on their stems. Darrius kicked the grasses and flowers convinced insects were causing the noise but found nothing. A chilly breeze swept by his cheek. Darrius shivered. Pimples dotted his arms. He stared at the curious bumps. Another human curiosity he'd study later.

Darkness descends. The voice rang louder this time and the humming ceased.

Darrius searched the meadow, unnerved by the stillness, but again found nothing. He grew tired of this game. He opened his mind.

If you are trying to communicate with me, then face me and talk with me. These whispers in my mind are games for children.

He took a chance hoping his words were not too harsh, and that they would prompt the entity to join him.

In the distance, a vibration rumbled up from deep beneath the mountain. Denali's heartbeat pulsed forward, racing across the valley toward Darrius. On the crest of the shockwave rode an intense energy—natural magic. As it roared across the meadow, the landscape sprang to life. All living things—the trees, the rocks, and even the beasts—sang the song of Denali. The air sizzled with charged electricity.

Snaps, pops, and clicks exploded around Darrius. The hairs on his body stood at attention, reaching for the magnetic energy crashing over him. Darrius glanced back to Stygian and the men. The soldiers bent their heads against another volley of insults from their leader. If they felt the strange energy, they gave no indication.

The small earthquake roiled under Darrius' boots. He wondered if this odd energy was a reply to his message. Were these vibrations and static charges a precursor to an entity's arrival?

Caw.

Glancing up, he saw a large raven skimming just overhead. The black bird flew toward Denali before banking to the right and circling the meadow. It returned to Darrius. This time the bird dipped low, its talons scraping across his head attempting to capture his attention. Intuition poked at Darrius. The raven flew off urging Darrius to follow it.

There was something remarkable about this creature. Its appearance coincided with the arrival of the strange vibrations. What if the key to understanding this land was to listen to the inhabitants living in this natural energy? Darrius gazed after the raven, following its flight. The bird suddenly dropped, landing on a monolithic boulder. The massive rock stood in a flood of purple lupines puddling down the valley toward Denali. The raven bobbed its head and cawed.

The warmth of understanding seeped across Darrius' mind. This boulder was significant, an important entity that shouldn't be ignored. Had this rock tried to communicate with him? As before, he opened his mind and reached out. He'd never mind-probed a solid object before. But this land, and its energy, was so different from Ceres.

Are you the being who reached out to me? Darrius waited. He quivered with excitement, but there was also an undercurrent of anxiety. Several moments passed before he received his reply.

Darkness descends.

Darrius sighed. Perhaps he didn't yet understand how to communicate with this being. He needed to try harder. After all, the entity chose him from the rest of the soldiers. There's an honor that accompanies that appointment...and a responsibility. Asking a different question might produce a different response. He faced the boulder and tried again.

What is the darkness? he asked.

The evil that arrived with you.

Chapter 2

Natural Magic

RIVULETS OF SWEAT TRICKLED down Stygian's head and the droplets lingered on his upper lip before sliding into his open mouth—a grimace sliced into his beet-red face. The pale-skinned Cererian trudged forward several yards ahead of his men. The Alaskan sun stoked his emotional fire poking the rage which simmered since his tirade a day earlier.

While their commander suffered in the summer heat, the soldiers and Darrius felt no ill effects. To them, the temperatures felt mild and the breezes were almost chilly. Darrius speculated that fusing their Cererian blood with human DNA prompted various reactions depending on the host body. But he wondered why Stygian would be suffering more than the others.

Darrius mulled over the voice's words, *"The evil that arrived with you."* Had they inadvertently brought something evil to Earth? Or had a malevolent virus hitched a ride on their spacecraft? At Darrius' insistence, Andee examined each soldier, collecting data on their physical and mental conditions.

"I am your commander and refuse to participate," Stygian protested.

Darrius anticipated his friend's response, "I don't need to remind you, Stygian, that our general expects daily transmissions. How would it appear if you're not participating?"

Stygian's face contorted as vicious thoughts raced through his mind. Finally, he relented. "I do this only for my general and nobody else." He scowled angrily at Darrius while Andee scanned his body.

Nothing unusual was found during the examinations. There were no foreign substances or organisms. But Andee noted one anomaly: Stygian's blood pressure was unusually high, and there was no known cause as to why it continued to escalate.

Andee confided in Darrius, "The high blood pressure may be contributing to the deterioration of Stygian's emotional state."

"Is there anything you can do?"

"No. But I will continue to monitor as much as the Commander allows." Andee dropped his head, a defeated look on his face. The beleaguered scientist grew weary of the continuous rebukes from his leader. "I doubt I'll be very successful, but I will try, Darrius."

Darrius managed a weak smile. "I appreciate your willingness to help."

"Let's move!" Stygian snapped, jerking his hand at the soldiers. "We need to find those humans!" He abruptly turned and marched off. The soldiers watched him disappear over a small hill before they gathered their instruments and followed. Distance is what everybody needed.

Darrius flanked the men. Once close friends, Darrius now provoked the worst from Stygian with the smallest action or word. For the sake of the soldiers, he kept his distance and the peace. Stygian didn't mind the separation. In fact, Darrius sensed he preferred it. Several attempts to mentally contact his friend went unanswered.

Throughout the day, Stygian kept to himself, brooding and mumbling. On occasion, he would explode with rage and stab the nearest tree with his battle dagger as though attacking an enemy. Accustomed to their leader's unusual actions, the soldiers continued to carry out their work while keeping a cautious eye on their commander.

While Thane and Everild searched the area for evidence of humans, Andee and Benedict gathered cellular samples of flowers, grasses, bushes, and trees.

"Ow!" Benedict yelled, jumping away from a frightening plant armed with spines from top to bottom. The hapless Cererian inadvertently grabbed its thorny stem while moving the plant aside.

Andee hovered over Benedict's hand, closely inspecting it. Tiny prickles clung to his fingers and part of his palm, appearing like a covering of fine brown hair on his pale white hands. Andee sighed. "It will be a tedious chore to remove all these little spines. How many times have I asked you to look first and touch later?"

"Dad, not now." Benedict hung his head embarrassed not only from his blunder but for being admonished by his father in front of the other soldiers. Benedict peered out from under his long white hair to see if the men were staring. Fortunately, his comrades had moved away and hadn't noticed the commotion.

Andee scanned the plant. "It's not poisonous, but your hand will throb for a while. It's called a devil's club." The tiny man looked up at his son who blushed a deep crimson. "It's okay Benedict, you know what do to next time. Let's get a sample and move on."

"Shh!"

The sharp command silenced everyone. Stygian hunched low by a tall thicket of trees and twisted his body toward the soldiers. He held a finger to his mouth while motioning for everyone to stop with his other hand. The men dropped to the ground and froze, their eyes fixed on their commander. They exchanged nervous looks as they awaited further orders.

Stygian heard voices. Human whispers. He leaned into the thicket, swiveling his head to locate the noise. Facing the men, he pointed to the other side of the trees and signaled for them to arm themselves and join him. The soldiers withdrew their battle daggers—curved, metal blades with vicious teeth angled forward and backward. The men could only use it in close proximity, but the foot-long weapon was lethal causing great damage going in and coming out.

Armed, the men duck-walked to their leader, mindful to stay low. Except for Darrius. Sensing no danger, he stood tall, and his weapon remained sheathed. His intuition recognized that whoever was on the other side of the woods would not harm them. Stygian scowled at his disobedience as he calmly joined the soldiers, acknowledging Stygian with a respectful nod.

"Follow me and stay close," Stygian ordered. Pushing the limbs aside, he cautiously worked his way through the thicket. The men followed, careful to step in his footprints.

SNAP!

A branch Stygian had bent to the side broke off in his hand. Everyone froze. Stygian's shoulders shuddered, his lips thinned, and his hands had balled into fists at his side. The men winced. They recognized the sign of an eruption, but they had nowhere to run.

Brother, you have brought us this far. Take us the rest of the way. Darrius' calm words drifted through his friend's mind.

Stygian drew in a strangled breath, holding it for several seconds before blowing it through clenched teeth. He stared at Darrius. For several moments, the two friends shared a gaze unfettered by accusations or blame.

The wave of anger slowly subsided, and Stygian turned away from Darrius. A hushed gasp of relief escaped the soldiers who had been holding their breaths expecting the worst from their leader. Without a word, Stygian plowed forward, carefully navigating the last twenty feet of the woods in silence.

Stygian emerged from the trees, his battle dagger leading the way as he ran into the clearing. The soldiers quickly followed, fanning out on both sides of him forming an arc with their weapons, hoping to surprise the humans. But the people they expected were not there.

It was a deserted village of twenty thatched huts.

The silence was disconcerting. Just moments earlier, Stygian had heard whispers and voices of multiple individuals. He sheathed his weapon and surveyed the area. Thick, old-growth forests bordered the village on all sides except for the small thicket of trees they had just passed through. A tribe of people could not escape that fast silently.

"Where did the humans go?" he whispered to himself, his forehead wrinkling in disbelief. Frustrated, he barked, "Search each home! Find the humans."

The soldiers dispersed into the village, checking each house for signs of life. The ten-foot square huts formed a loose circle around an enormous fire constructed with thick logs. A black cauldron rested in the middle of the blaze; a thick stew swirled inside.

Everild examined the wood and then the contents of the pot. "Commander, this fire has not burned for very long. Fifteen minutes at the most."

Andee, Benedict, and Thane explored the homes. They entered unannounced, yanking the simple cloth covering away from the doorways. They found bedding and clothes, but no humans.

"There's nobody in the huts, Commander," Thane reported. "Dinner has been prepared, but everyone is gone."

Something was amiss. Stygian mulled over the signs—the huts, the campfire, the food—everything was perfectly in place, indicating people had been here recently. So, where did they vanish to and how? His fingers tapped the handle of his dagger as he considered the possibilities. Suddenly he withdrew his weapon and cried out, "This is a trap!"

The words barely escaped his lips, when a foreign voice hailed them.

"Hello! Whom do we have here?"

The Cererians whirled, their weapons gripped in their hands. They crouched low, ready to spring forward. But no monster stood before them.

A young man stood atop a boulder several yards away. A bright smile filled his face, popping dimples in his tanned cheeks.

Sandy, brown hair fluttered in the breeze, while his vivid blue eyes sparkled with joy. He wore a simple white muslin shirt, a deer hide vest fell low to his hips, and black cotton breeches gathered at the knee. He wore no shoes, and his blackened toenails gripped the edges of the boulder deftly as a mountain goat on Denali's cliffs.

"Who are you?" Stygian growled.

The human stared at the odd group of men, gazing from one man to the next before he replied, "I asked you first, stranger."

Darrius studied the young man. He appeared non-threatening. But his posture also indicated that he was alert and ready to react to anything. Darrius saw no weapon, but his intuition suggested this creature possessed immense power and would use it if attacked.

Angered by the human's smug response, Stygian curled his lips. "You..."

Darrius spoke over Stygian, smothering his terse reply. "We are visitors here. We have traveled a great distance and only seek food. We don't mean any harm."

Darrius stepped beside Stygian and gently placed a hand on his shoulder. *Forgive me, friend, patience is warranted right now.* Stygian glared at Darrius, but acquiesced to his suggestion, remembering their mission was to engage the inhabitants.

The young man studied the short daggers in the fists of the soldiers. "Your actions tell me otherwise."

"Ah, but we were surprised by your announcement. You will note that we did not jump forward and attack you. We waited to see what kind of person you were."

The human chuckled. His hearty laugh rolled for several seconds as though he recalled a private joke. Poking his chin at Darrius, he continued, "You're different from the others. Your aura is brilliant, not dull like the rest of these men."

"How dare you," Stygian hissed. His eyes narrowed and his teeth clenched.

Darrius sensed Stygian's anger building and messaged his friend. *Remember, brother, do not lose your patience. This is not the place or the time.*

The stranger nodded. "I agree with your friend, warrior, this is not the place or the time for negative actions."

Darrius' eyebrows arched with surprise at the stranger's ability to capture his telepathic thoughts to Stygian. He moved closer attempting to probe the unusual man.

"You, too, are extraordinary. I sense a peculiar energy surrounding you. It's as though you're a wispy image and not a solid form. Like you're a spirit."

The young man beamed, neither agreeing nor denying Darrius' observation. He gazed into the face of each man, lingering for several moments before returning to Darrius.

"Your aura beats strong, stranger. But, underneath your exterior, I know you are not who you appear to be."

Darrius cringed internally, careful to not let his face betray his feelings. Was this human detecting their fake personas?

The man swiftly adjusted his stance, hopping gleefully on the boulder in a small circle. Unsure of the stranger's intentions, the soldiers cocked their heads at the bizarre display. The young man's eyes twinkled with mischief as he grinned at the Cererians who appeared quite confused by his actions. Relishing their befuddlement, the stranger stopped and spread his arms wide.

"Welcome to my world. The world of Denali." Stunned by the sudden shift in his behavior, the Cererians gawked at the human, questioning his sanity. "My name is Manx." He pointed toward the distant mountain peak. "Our earth mother, Denali, showers us with love and abundance. I am happy to share our wealth with all of you."

Manx was not insane. He had purposely altered his behavior to distract the Cererians. The magical young man channeled Denali's positive energy and pushed it toward the soldiers, hoping to disarm their negative intentions. The calming wave crashed over the men in a cooling burst of charged air. The effects were immediate. Battle daggers fell to the ground as the men hung their heads, their sleepy eyes slowly opening and closing. Even Stygian visibly relaxed. His tense sneer transformed into an impassive smile. The shift in energy created a warm and welcoming environment.

Darrius cordially introduced himself. "I am Darrius and this is my colleague, Stygian—"

"Wealth? You mentioned wealth," Stygian interrupted Darrius in a hoarse whisper. His head bobbed and he struggled to keep his eyes open.

Manx chuckled, cupping his mouth with his hand. "I don't mean to laugh at you stranger but our wealth is this land and the energy that flows from Denali through all the living things—nature's spirits, magicians and Folk."

"Folk? This is a new term for me," Darrius mentioned.

The Harvesters had advised that the soldiers would adopt the innate abilities of their host bodies. Darrius suspected his donor either possessed magic or was impervious to the effects. Unlike the other soldiers, Darrius was not affected by Manx's spell. The speed at which it affected the Cererians was unsettling, but the magic didn't appear to be harming anyone.

Darrius decided to see what the young man had to offer. He was very curious about this creature's powers.

Manx eagerly responded, "Our land is comprised of those with magic and those who do not have extraordinary gifts. Although we are different in our abilities, we all contribute equally to our community."

Stygian staggered a few steps closer to the young man. "Are you the leader?" He attempted to probe Manx's mind. Cererian scientists had advised telepathy would be easy to perform on humans, but this young man was different. Manx blocked Stygian's efforts.

Manx chuckled again. The sound was like the rich melody from a little bell. "I am not. We have a Council comprised of members of all the families. Together, they make decisions based on the needs of our community."

"We need to talk to your Council," Stygian insisted. A frown fluttered across Manx's face as though the brusque demand had slapped his cheek.

Noticing Manx's displeased reaction, Darrius added, "Would it be okay if we could visit your village and meet with the Council?"

That's not what I meant, Darrius! Stygian mentally yelled at Darrius. *I tire of you shoving words in my mouth.*

Stygian, please, remember our mission.

Manx smiled. The corners of his eyes softly crinkled. *In my culture we block our thoughts when we're having a private conversation.* Embarrassed, the two Cererians blinked at Manx who seemed somewhat pleased with having surprised them with his ability.

"Forgive our insensitive behavior," Darrius blurted. "I forgot you possess the gift of telepathy. We meant no disrespect."

"Your apology is graciously accepted." Manx nodded at Darrius assuring him everything was fine. He suddenly tilted his head and closed his eyes as though he was intently listening to something or someone. After several moments he spoke, "My apologies, I must leave you. I'm being summoned."

"May we join you?" Darrius felt awkward asking the question but was intrigued by this young man. If there was an opportunity to meet more of his kind, it promised to be an enriching encounter.

Manx clasped his hands in front of his chest, his fingertips tapping together as he considered Darrius' question before he abruptly replied, "No. I must take my leave of you." As he uttered the words, he slowly lifted his arms out to either side and snapped his fingers.

His body vanished.

"Damn the stars!" Stygian yelled, racing to the boulder. He bounded on top just as the last molecules disappeared. "We had him. We could have easily taken the human. But Darrius had to cajole and placate the stranger. And now he's gone!" Stygian paced back and forth. With Manx's departure, the calming energy dissolved and Stygian welcomed the return of his anger with open arms. He suddenly kicked Benedict in his backside, sending the hapless young man sprawling into the dirt. Then he faced Darrius with eyes darkened with rage. "Darrius, if you ever humiliate me again, you and I will have a serious situation."

Darrius stared at his friend, unblinking. Several tense moments passed before Stygian broke the standoff and barked at his soldiers, "Search the huts again. There may be clues hidden in them."

"Commander, something's very wrong," Thane announced, pointing toward the village.

Stygian followed the soldier's gaze and gasped. "What? This is not possible!"

The small circle of huts and blazing fire had vanished. The soldiers stared in amazement at a large, blue lake, its waves gently lapping onto the shore where the men stood.

"Split up and check the shoreline!" Stygian ordered. "That human is playing with us!"

Thane and Everild went left while Andee and Benedict checked the area to the right. The soldiers met on the other side of the lake. They found nothing, not even a footprint.

"We found no evidence of the village, Commander," Benedict reported.

"I can see that, idiot!" Stygian backhanded him. Benedict fell to the ground, holding his mouth. Blood coated his teeth. Andee knelt by his side and gently dabbed his son's lips while nervously glancing up at his commander. Towering over the two men, Stygian clenched his fists, fighting the urge to stomp the two soldiers to death.

"Brother!" The word was sharp but not mean-spirited. Darrius wedged himself between Stygian and the men. He forcibly moved his friend, pushing him several yards away. "Brother, look at me." It took all of Darrius' strength to restrain Stygian, but he wouldn't let go of his friend, he couldn't let him attack the soldiers. "Brother?" Concern filled his voice as Darrius peered into his friend's eyes which had turned black, the pupils fully dilated.

Stygian pulled away and growled a low warning, "Darrius, this is not the time." The Cererian hunched over like an angry bear his head twisting side to side, furiously jerking his arms to be free of Darrius' grip, but his friend would not let him go.

"Brother, please look at me," Darrius implored. If he could establish a good connection with Stygian's eyes, Darrius had a chance to sedate his friend through trancing.

"I know what you're doing, Darrius," Stygian yelled, wrenching his head to the side. "You are not going to hypnotize me!"

A vicious gust of wind suddenly knocked the men to the ground. As they scrambled to their feet, Darrius gripped Stygian in a bearhug. Now they were face to face. Darrius had a chance to deploy his hypnotic powers. Before he could act, a cyclone appeared overhead. The anomaly startled everyone since there were no clouds in the sky except for this dark gray, moaning mass of turbulent wind. Growling and groaning, the small tornado slowly descended over the fighting Cererians.

Though the winds buffeted them viciously, there was hardly a breeze outside its perimeter. Benedict noted, "Father, the plant leaves are not fluttering, yet the clothes on Stygian and Darrius are being torn to shreds inside the cyclone."

The men clung to each other as the tornado lifted them from the ground, twirling them in circles.

"What bizarre spawn of weather is this!" Andee shouted as he ran under the spinning funnel, the boots of the men dangling just feet above his head. He jumped to grab Darrius' foot and pull him out of the vortex. "Thane...Everild...Benedict...help me!" The men huddled under the violent cyclone, leaping up to grab a foot or a leg, only to have the windstorm yank its victims away. After several minutes, the tornado abruptly dissipated. It's gray, wispy clouds spiraled upward into the clear blue sky until it simply vanished. Darrius and Stygian dropped to the ground with a thump.

Physically drained, the two friends lay on the ground gasping for breath while the soldiers bustled around them checking for wounds. The healer in the group, Andee, examined Stygian first and then Darrius noting that besides being a little breathless, they had no injuries, not even a scratch.

"What was that?" Darrius wheezed, struggling into a sitting position.

"We weren't warned about that kind of creature!" Stygian snarled.

Studying his handheld device, Andee punched in data before proclaiming, "Unless our information is incorrect, this type of tornadic occurrence is an unknown anomaly, never before seen on Earth."

"It's as though somebody intervened in our quarrel," Darrius suggested. His eyes drifted over the landscape. He expected to see Manx dancing in the distance. Then he felt it. The energy shifted as though a heartbeat vibration passed through him. A gentle humming snatched his attention. Darrius looked to the others. "Did you hear that?"

The soldiers shook their heads. Thane and Everild helped Stygian stand and brushed the dirt from his uniform. Darrius turned away from the men and looked back to the boulder where Manx had first appeared. His intuition spoke to him, insisting that the source of the energy he felt was nearby. The humming intensified. Darrius titled his head. He could hear words. Yes, there were distinct words within the thrumming. He glanced back at the soldiers who had moved away toward the lake, leaving him alone.

A strong compulsion coaxed Darrius to focus on the towering peak in the distance—Denali. The magnetic pull was incredibly strong. Fascinated by the energy swirling around him, Darrius allowed himself to be drawn into the energy current. The buzzing increased causing him to feel light-headed almost euphoric.

Natural magic. The voice whispered into his brain.

His eyes flashed with excitement. He reached out with his mind as he did with the giant boulder when they entered the valley. But first, he would block his thoughts from the others in his party. *Who are you?* he asked it.

I am all life. I am the trees, the water, the creatures, the sky, the air that you breathe. I am you.

Darrius sighed. The vagueness had returned, and it was more confusing than before. Frustrated, Darrius pressed, *Please tell me who you are.*

Natural magic. You'll feel my warmth in the rays of the morning sun. You'll smell my perfume in the heads of fragrant flowers. You'll taste the bitterness on your tongue from the unripe berries. Your life will feel joy, sorrow, happiness, and sadness; and one day you will sleep comfortably in your earthen chamber, in the bosom of your earth mother.

Manx spoke about an earth mother, Denali. Was this the spirit of the mountain that hailed Darrius now? *Are you the earth spirit the humans call Denali?*

An intense silence descended upon the land. If this was Denali, why would she reach out to him? Why contact a Cererian?

We, the spirits of nature, are ever vigilant of the doings of man. We are well aware of your arrival, star visitor, and are mindful of your impact on this wondrous planet of ours. You are different.

Your energy glows brighter than the rest. We're aware of your forced transformation to be in our world. But you, you among the others have transformed with the DNA of a shaman, a holy man who once walked with the Elementals. You carry a modicum of what he possessed, but he pulses freely in your veins and will soon dominate your natural inclinations. Natural magic.

I don't understand. Your riddles confuse me.

Know this. When you arrived in our world, the spirits rejoiced. But your brilliant light will always entice the darker energies intent on snuffing out your brightness. The day you arrived evil also set foot upon our land.

Evil? We brought no evil with us. Our intentions are benevolent. We mean no harm.

Trust your intuition. Things are not as they appear.

Abruptly, a series of vibrations crashed over Darrius, tossing him around as though he weighed nothing. The shockwaves left him disoriented and woozy. His stomach gurgled, and he felt the urge to be sick. As he stumbled toward a bush to vomit, Andee grabbed his arm. "Darrius! Are you okay?"

Darrius shook his head trying to clear the cobwebs from his mind. He couldn't tell Andee about his discussion with a spirit. Andee would think he was experiencing a mental breakdown and might quarantine him. "I guess I'm still suffering the effects of that rogue tornado," he lied.

"I ask because you stared at that mountain in the distance for five minutes and never once blinked." Andee studied Darrius evaluating his behavior and reactions.

"Did I? I don't remember." Darrius glanced over the valley, lingering on Denali. "There's something magical about this place."

Andee followed his gaze. "I agree. Odd things occur here. Regarding the village that was here and then vanished, I researched possible reasons for its disappearance, and it may have been a mirage. Apparently, they are quite frequent if the weather conditions are right."

"Perhaps," Darrius said. "Maybe our mirage may decide to return. Or perhaps our magical emissary watches us even now." Darrius whirled to look at the rock where Manx first introduced himself.

"Come on, Andee, let's join the others in setting up the camp. We need to get an early start tomorrow."

Thane and Everild erected the tents while Benedict and Andee built a fire and began preparing food. Stygian stood several yards away, intensely staring at the lake, willing the village to reappear. The muscles in his jaw bunched as he mulled over the unusual occurrences of the day.

Darrius almost pitied his brother. He couldn't imagine the emotional turmoil roiling in his blood. The outbursts and the fury grew more intense. Yet, Darrius grew calmer with each passing day. The two friends had embarked on two diverse journeys.

It wasn't long before Darrius allowed his mind to wander back to the recent conversation with the earth spirit. He was sure it was Denali, although the entity never admitted its identity. *This land really is magical. Things are not as they appear. I wonder if Manx is even a human or is he just another mirage?* he pondered.

I can assure you I am human.

The response surprised Darrius and he jerked to his right convinced Manx was standing next to him whispering in his ear. But nobody was there. His eyes darted to his comrades wondering if they had noticed anything. But they busied themselves around camp. He glanced at Stygian who still maintained his vigil on the lakeshore.

Darrius opened his mind. *How are you able to do what you do, if you're not a spirit?*

Natural magic.

Chapter 3

The Welcoming

A WARM, SWEET SCENT flowed over the Cererians as they slept. Like wisps of smoke, the floral scent snaked between the soldiers, infusing their clothes and hair with hints of honey sweetness.

Benedict moaned with pleasure. He lingered on the fringe of a dream fueled by the aroma and envisioned himself eating breakfast porridge with gooey swirls of golden nectar. He bolted awake, drool sliding down his chin. He swiped it with the back of his hand as he closed his eyes relishing the last remnants of the tasty dream fleeing into the deep recesses of his mind. He inhaled long and deep. The intoxicating scent beckoned him.

"I see they woke you as well," his father whispered.

"Who do you mean?"

"The lupines. We passed a field of them on our journey to this spot. The aroma prompted my dream of the sugar vines that grew near our home on Ceres."

"I was dreaming as well. Only I was in my human body, and I was doling sweet nectar into my porridge."

Andee chuckled. "This land is truly enchanted. After the visit from Manx, the unexplained tornado, and the village that vanished, I'm not sure what we'll encounter today. But I promise you, it will be extraordinary." He winked and patted his son's back. "Now, let's get the fire roaring and prepare food for our comrades."

Not long after, the rest of the men awoke. Thane and Everild walked the perimeter inspecting the boundary, which was infused with intruder alert magic. They carefully checked the connections for any abnormalities. Finding the area secure, the soldiers joined Andee and Benedict. They ate their breakfast in silence except for the occasional sniff in the air as each man inhaled the inviting scent of the lupines.

Darrius sat on a log across the fire from Stygian. He chewed slowly while studying his friend. Despite Andee's attempts, Stygian had denied further examinations. So Darrius took it upon himself to assess his brother frequently. He maintained a private log of his observations, hoping the information would, one day, prove beneficial to his general. He wasn't the only one evaluating Stygian. Due to his volatile fury, which was meted on every soldier without prejudice, each man spent considerable time measuring their commander's temperament. Their constant, guarded behavior only increased their stress.

Darrius rose and stretched. Stygian observed him with an alert eye. Suspicion festered in his soul. His mistrust of everyone contributed to his escalating anxiety.

"I'm going to check out the surrounding area," Darrius announced while grabbing his backpack.

"Don't stray too far, Darrius," Stygian cautioned. "We leave in one hour."

Darrius nodded, mindful to avoid provoking his friend. "I'll be back in time. I won't be out of sight as I circle the camp."

After examining the boulder where they encountered Manx, Darrius followed the shoreline around the lake, scanning for any evidence of the village that existed the day before. Holding his hand parallel to the ground, Darrius opened his mind to receive whatever information he could, but there was nothing conclusive about the elusive community.

A sharp squeak stopped him in his tracks.

The odd sound didn't register as anything he'd ever heard. It was like a bird, but also sounded like metal rubbing together. He surveyed the area—his gaze swept across the water, along the forests, and back to camp. Nothing was out of order. He sighed and resumed walking forward.

"Watch it!"

Darrius leapt back with his arms raised, ready for combat. Manx stood six feet away, a wry smile snaked across his brown face and playfulness danced in his eyes.

"You startled me!" A wave of relief coursed through Darrius' body. He yearned to learn more about this young man.

"Are you up for an adventure?" Manx turned to leave. Darrius grabbed his shoulder and stopped him. Manx cocked his head and peered at the Cererian. Darrius stared back, doubt darkening his eyes. "Ah, you were expecting me to be a mirage." Manx chuckled as he tapped his chest, "As you can see, I'm real." He twirled and sauntered toward the lake.

Darrius was unsure about following. This beguiling creature confused him with his playfulness and impetuous behavior. But his curiosity plucked at him to follow the magician and learn about him. The young man waited at the water's edge and waved his hand, inviting Darrius to join him. "Come on, Darrius. We won't be gone long." Manx's blue eyes sparkled in the sunshine like a beacon of pleasure.

Darrius glanced back to the camp almost a hundred yards away. Regretfully, he declined. "I can't. I promised the others I would stay within sight."

"Very well, so you shall," Manx chirped he rejoined the Cererian. He wrapped his arm around Darrius' waist. "Please join me, an adventure awaits."

A personal invitation to explore this young man's world was hard to resist. Darrius considered all he would see and learn, including magic. He wondered if Manx would reveal the identity of the spirits who spoke with him recently. That alone excited him. But he had promised his comrades he would always be within sight of the camp.

He studied Manx's face—youthful innocence with a twist of naughtiness. How could he resist this handsome, magical creature?

Darrius nodded. "Yes, I'd love to join you. But how will I remain visible to my comrades?"

"Trust me, Darrius." Manx gripped Darrius' hand and gently tugged. Darrius didn't resist and allowed Manx to pull him forward toward the water's edge. The two men stood side by side, staring across the lake. A thick fog slowly descended and swirled over the surface, the water disappearing under its white veil. Manx gazed at the mist and casually asked, "Do you swim?"

"What?" The word barely escaped Darrius' lips when Manx pushed him headfirst into the lake.

The plunge into the frigid water shocked his system and he floundered in the chest-high water, struggling to find his footing. Thrashing his arms and cursing Manx, Darrius finally slogged to shore. His drenched clothes smoldered as steam drifted up into the moist, chilly air. He shivered violently and hugged himself while glaring at Manx who remained in the lake, a faint smile gracing his lips. Darrius felt betrayed.

"Why did you do that?"

"Do what?" In a second, the lake vanished, and the two men stood on the outskirts of a small village surrounded by ancient woods. Darrius gaped at the scene before him—houses, streets, people, and animals. Was this a mirage? He squeezed his eyes shut. He slowly opened one eye and then the other. But it was still there. The thriving community of almost a hundred souls stretched out before him. He patted his clothes. What was soaking wet moments before was now dry. How was this possible?

Darrius nervously looked around. There was no sign of his camp or even the lake. "You promised I'd still be visible to my comrades!"

Manx tilted his head to one side. "Ah, but you are still visible to them. You have not left the lakeshore at all. You, my curious friend, are standing in both worlds at this very moment."

Darrius thought Manx was mad. But he couldn't deny what his eyes were seeing. People hailed them as they passed as though it was natural to see a stranger in their midst. "So the village never disappeared? You've been here all the time?"

Manx laughed out loud. "Exactly! Natural Magic!"

"I've been hearing that a lot lately. What exactly does that mean?"

"Why don't we stroll as I try to explain." Manx took Darrius' arm and led him around the village, introducing him to various people, explaining how they collect energy from the sun's rays and demonstrating how the magic of each household contributes to the survival of the community. The inhabitants opened their hearts and homes to Darrius, welcoming him as though he was one of their own.

"Hungry?" Manx invited Darrius to sit at a long, wooden table outside an establishment serving food and drink. Above the door, a plank sign dangled by two strands of rope. Images of a beer mug and fruit decorated both sides in muted colors of yellow, red, and green.

Baxter, the proprietor, approached and slapped Manx on the back. "I like your friend, Manx. He's authentic." He turned to Darrius. "Here friend, have an ale on me."

Darrius beamed. "Thank you. I feel so welcome here." Darrius then turned to Manx and whispered, "I haven't formally met him yet. How does he know I'm 'authentic.'"

Manx exploded with laughter. His infectious chuckle attracted the attention of the patrons who smiled at the duo. Their stares were too much for Darrius who blushed and cast his eyes down to the table, hoping to hide his embarrassment. Manx noticed Darrius' uneasiness and leaned close. He spoke softly, his breathy whisper tickling the tiny hairs inside Darrius' ear.

"My dear Darrius. Don't be sad. Your naivety is so refreshing. You're just beginning to flex the emotional and physical muscles of your human body. Allow your natural urges to come forward." A broad grin suddenly flashed across his face, popping both dimples. "In our world, energy is a constant. Baxter saw and felt your energy, and knew you were genuine, as do all these people." Manx threw his arms wide gesturing toward the various couples sitting nearby.

Their private conversation was interrupted by two giggling girls, wearing blue ribbons in their blonde, curly hair. At eight and nine, Baxter's daughters were young but old enough to share the responsibilities of running their family's business. They carefully placed two wooden plates of bread and fruit onto the table and then stepped back. They stared at Darrius, gawking at the Cererian from head to toe and back up again before they turned to each other whispering and giggling.

"Girls, it's not polite to stare," Manx noted softly as he chewed a slice of bread.

The girls giggled again. "But he's so different, Manx. He's beautiful like a winter's night."

Manx looked at Darrius, studying him with one eyebrow arched. "I see what you mean. Now off you go before you make him feel uncomfortable." The two girls ran away, their giggles trailing behind them.

Darrius watched the girls disappear, enchanted by their cute, childish behavior. He turned to Manx. "A winter's night? What does that mean?"

Manx leaned back and stroked his smooth chin. "They offered you a rich compliment, my friend. There is no comparable beauty to the night sky during midwinter—a luscious blackness adorned with sparkling jewels and the brilliant greens of the Aurora Borealis. Hopefully, you stay with us long enough to experience it."

A warm smile lingered on Darrius' face as he regarded the simple comparison of his appearance to one of nature's beautiful sights.

The two men ate in silence for several minutes until Darrius asked, "Why did you invite me?"

Manx refilled Darrius' mug with a long pour of amber ale before responding, "As I told you yesterday. You're different from the others in your camp. Your aura shines bright. But I know you're not mortal, that you reside in a body crafted from harvested DNA."

Darrius flinched at his words as though they were armed with tiny daggers. He detested the clinical description of his body. Hearing Manx's explanation, Darrius felt like a body thief. Over the last nine days, he had grown accustomed to the workings of his human form. He marveled at the power of his heart, pumping blood throughout his veins and his lungs inflating with each breath sending much-needed oxygen into the brain. Experiencing all the senses—sight, sound, smell, hearing and touch—allowed him to plunge into a new world of awareness. And it excited him to explore these new feelings. "How do you know so much about me?"

"Your arrival was foretold to us."

"By whom?"

Manx changed the subject. "Your scientists have done an incredible job pairing your brilliant energy with your exceptional body." The genuine praise surprised Darrius. A warmth seeped throughout his body and a new emotion—shyness—crept in. He felt vulnerable and unsure how to respond to Manx. He stared into his mug of ale searching the amber fluid for the right words. Manx reached over and impulsively stroked Darrius' cheek. Darrius trembled with delight. Manx's fingertip felt like a warm ray of sunshine on his face. He lifted his head and gazed at Manx. "And those incredible green eyes. I would willingly drown in their emerald sea."

The two men searched each other's faces, sensing intentions. Primal feelings rushed upward. Their hearts galloped. Their breaths quickened. Slowly, Manx bent closer until his lips found Darrius'. He stopped, hovering over Darrius' bottom lip, teasing it with his tongue as he scanned Darrius' eyes for permission to continue. A tremendous warmth exploded in Darrius' lower belly, and he sighed before crushing against Manx, kissing him long and hard. Their tongues flicked and probed, igniting a welcome heat that consumed their thoughts and actions. Breathless, they pulled away and gazed at each other. Darrius' mind raced. These were new feelings, very delightful feelings.

"Well, that was delicious!" Manx exclaimed. He propped his elbows on the table and rested his head on his hands. He playfully looked at Darrius with puppy dog eyes.

"I don't know what to say..." Darrius stammered.

"Did you like it?"

"Very much."

"Do you want to kiss me again?"

"Very much." Darrius lightly stroked Manx's cheek, sliding a finger along the tender skin before moving it along the ridge of his nose. Darrius kissed him, gently sucking on his top lip before his tongue thrust deep, parting his mouth. Darrius pressed harder into Manx, gripping him in a tender hug, sliding his hand to his lower back, and pulling him closer.

Manx suddenly pulled away.

"Did I do something wrong?" Darrius searched his face, anxious that he may have harmed him.

Manx smiled and rose. His eyes sparkled with joy. He grabbed Darrius' hand and pulled him up. "Ready for your adventure? I know I am." Manx giggled.

Darrius nodded, eagerly following Manx as the young man led him to his house—a modest, two-room home. Sandalwood incense wafted as Manx led Darrius into the main room which featured a hearth in the middle, surrounded by massive multi-colored pillows. Against the wall stood a small table with several bottles containing liquids of purple, red, and yellow. Manx poured the contents into two glasses, forming a rainbow, layered drink. "Come Darrius, join me on the pillows," he said handing one glass to Darrius.

Darrius held the glass up, examining the different swirls of color. "This is very interesting. What is this drink?"

"This is a day of many firsts for you, my friend. This drink possesses the spirits of various plants from our land. You'll taste elderberry, fireweed, and some bitter notes concocted from dandelion flowers. Combined they are delicious but potent."

Darrius took a short sip, allowing the liquor to slide throughout his mouth. An explosion of exotic flavors flowed over his tongue before disappearing down his throat in one smooth gulp. His pupils suddenly enlarged. "This is exceptional!" He eagerly tilted the glass and consumed the entire contents, using his tongue to capture any lingering drops.

Somewhat shocked, Manx sputtered, "Well, I was going to tell you to take it easy with the drink, but I guess I'm too late." The two men laughed as Manx refilled their glasses. An hour passed.

Darrius relaxed against Manx, resting his head on his shoulder. Manx nuzzled his curly hair and inhaled deeply. An alluring scent of musk and pheromones teased his thoughts and ignited an inner heat. Manx's tongue traced the edges of Darrius' ear.

Manx stood. Taking Darrius' hands, he pulled him up and passionately kissed him. Darrius sighed. He released the reins on his intuition, allowing it to run free and control his actions. Manx cupped his buttocks and pulled him closer. Darrius responded by grabbing Manx around the waist and crushing hard against his firmness. An explosion of heat and lust surged throughout his body.

Manx pushed back and grinned. "Come with me, my Darrius." The two men walked into the bedroom. "Now, don't move. Let me do everything." Silently, Manx undressed Darrius, first removing his shirt and then sliding his pants to the floor. "You have a remarkably strong body, Darrius," Manx whispered as he slid his fingertips across the Cererian's smooth, mocha chest and then down across his abdomen, circling his bellybutton before sliding his hand between his legs.

Darrius gasped, the breath catching in his throat. "Oh..." Manx smiled. Darrius had never felt so alive, so human. He yearned for more. "These feelings," Darrius panted. "I can't explain these feelings."

"Just let them come," Manx urged as he slowly undressed in front of Darrius. Darrius' tongue flicked over his lips as each article of clothing fell to the floor. His hands twitched, anxious to touch the gorgeous body standing before him. "Come here, Darrius." Darrius rushed into Manx's arms, eager to kiss the beautiful magician, anxious to explore his body. Manx licked the beads of sweat from Darrius' chest until he found a nipple and swirled it gently. Then he suckled softly as Darrius threw his head back and moaned. "That's right, Darrius. Give in to the pleasure."

Manx suddenly pulled away. He slowly walked to the bed and laid back, his legs dangling off the edge. Holding his arms out to the Cererian, he beckoned, "Come to me, my Darrius."

Emotions raced as Darrius stood between the magician's legs, staring at the beautiful body which was covered with black tattoos. He knelt on the floor and gently traced one of the symbols located on the Manx's stomach. "I recognize this marking from the star books I studied."

Manx moaned with pleasure. "Touch another one, please." Darrius traced an astrological sign tattooed on Manx's lower belly. The magician whimpered. Darrius traced several other markings, moving faster and faster until Manx suddenly shuddered, a strangled gasp escaping his mouth. "Oh...my...Darrius!"

"I don't know why, but I feel compelled to feed upon you. Is this normal for humans?"

Manx smiled and sat up to face him. He tenderly caressed Darrius' face. "You are awakening to your needs, Darrius. Please feed upon me as you are compelled to do. Trust your intuition." Manx placed a hand on either side of Darrius' head and kissed him gently on the forehead before guiding him forward and down to his lower belly. The magician fell backward onto the bed and watched his companion descend upon him like a starved man. Darrius sucked while Manx twirled the fine curly hair peppering the Cererian's head. "You are so lovely, my Darrius. Welcome to my world."

Chapter 4

The Invitation

DARRIUS JOLTED AWAKE. ONE moment he was lying with Manx, and now he stood in thigh-high frigid water, fully clothed. *What strange magic is this? Where's Manx?* He slapped the water to see if it was real. A chilly spray smacked his face. The lake was not a mirage. Why did Manx send him back to this world?

Memories of their time together lingered. Despite the cold water, Darrius was quite warm, and his heart hammered, thinking of the young man and his gentle touch. A lingering scent of sandalwood hung on his clothes and hair. Darrius breathed deeply, hoping to propel himself back into Manx's arms and into his bed.

"Darrius!" The harsh cry jerked the Cererian out of his pleasant daydream. He knew that voice and the man attached to it—Stygian. "Why are you standing in the water?"

Darrius realized why Manx suddenly sent him back to this world. Stygian had been looking for him. Darrius shook his head, clearing the confusion, hoping Stygian hadn't been probing his mind.

"Hello, Stygian." A wave of guilt passed through him, although he didn't fully understand the new emotion. As Manx had told him: *Today is a day of firsts for you!*

"Why are you in the water, Darrius? Did you find something?" Darrius wanted to tell his friend about the magical world on the other side but knew he couldn't share that information and jeopardize Manx and the villagers. Guilt pinged his stomach again. As a Cererian, his world was black and white and his answer should be truthful. But in this human body, with these new feelings, there was so much gray area to consider.

"Nothing significant." Darrius trudged to the shoreline. "I thought I would go further into the water to see if I could detect anything left behind by the village."

"And?" Stygian's clipped response indicated he was in no mood for drawn out replies.

"I found nothing," Darrius lied. Dishonesty. There it was again, that new trait in his arsenal as a human. This behavior was unthinkable for a Cererian, and yet, he found it so easy to do.

A bright flash filled the sky, followed immediately by a deafening roar. The ground shook violently under their feet. In the distance, a large thunderstorm boiled, flowing down the lower regions of Denali like an immense black cat prowling for prey. The approaching storm distracted Stygian from completing his interrogation of Darrius. "The weather on this planet is extreme and unpredictable. We'd better return to camp."

A cold gust buffeted the men as they ran back to their comrades. The blackened shelf cloud growled overhead. Behind it, a sheet of gray covered the valley as torrential rain poured from the sky. The men reached the tents just as the hail fell. The small pellets soon turned to large boulders of ice that pummeled their campsite. Anyone caught outside in the maelstrom would have perished, but the men were protected in their tents constructed of a Cererian metal mesh. Bonded together in several dense layers, the fabric was immensely durable.

Darrius's mind bounded between the enjoyable time spent with Manx in his magical realm to the ferocious storm grumbling overhead. This country was a paradox—an alluring land offering unique, wonderful gifts and a dangerous place waiting to kill. He eyed Stygian who hunched near the doorway of their tent intently watching the storm. He and his comrade were changing, transforming into new beings. As the Harvesters had warned, they were adapting to the emotions and physical nuances of their host bodies. If Darrius was evolving into a being who embraced the pleasures of the world, was Stygian opening up to its wickedness? Was Stygian the evil that had arrived on Earth?

"The storm has finally passed." There was an air of impatience in Stygian's voice. He burst from the tent like a wild creature escaping its cage.

The gray clouds raced to the horizon with white, spider veins of lightning. "What an unusual occurrence," Benedict observed, checking the camp for damage.

"This land is very odd, indeed," his father agreed. "Many things are not as they appear. Our leaders will be very happy with the data we've collected." Holding his hand at an angle, Andee vaporized a portion of a large hailstone that had wedged in with a group of rocks. The molecules funneled into a storage chamber on Andee's hip. With this efficient method of collecting samples of flora and fauna, Andee could easily catalog thousands of samples in a short time. Thane and Everild marched the perimeter, collecting items that had blown away during the fury and repairing the intruder alert boundary.

"Darrius, walk with me." Stygian's abrupt request bothered Darrius, an uneasy feeling slithering up his spine. He watched his friend march away, not waiting for a response. Stygian expected simple obedience.

Darrius reluctantly followed instinctively knowing his friend intended to continue the questioning he began at the lake. Stygian stopped near the boulder and stared off into the distance. He squinted against the sun as he scanned the horizon, searching for something. "This land is enchanted, is it not?"

Darrius's eyebrows arched in surprise. This didn't sound like his friend. Why would he ask such a question?

Stygian glared at Darrius. "Did you hear me?"

"I heard you, but the question seemed more like a statement and less like a question."

Stygian nodded. He looked off into the distance again. "That odd storm, the tornado that lifted us from the ground, and the magician we encountered yesterday. All unusual experiences..." His voice trailed off as though something more important had captured his attention.

Darrius frowned. *Where is this leading?*

"This morning, I found you in the middle of the lake with no explanation." Stygian faced Darrius. "We've been friends a very long time Darrius. I know when you're withholding information."

Darrius's stomach lurched, sweat beaded on his brow, and his hands grew clammy. Guilt. The annoying human feeling had returned. He collected his thoughts and calmly replied, "What do you want to know, Stygian?"

"I observed you walking the perimeter collecting data, but you stopped on the shore and faced the lake. What did you see?"

Darrius's mind raced. He couldn't reveal anything about the village. He couldn't betray Manx and the existence of the second world. Stygian placed a hand on his shoulder, his long thumbnail puncturing deep into the muscle. He smirked at Darrius's grimace.

"What did you see, Darrius?"

What could he say? How could he respond? His heart thumped and he gulped for air as his human body fought the rising panic. Stygian pushed his nail deeper into the muscle and Darrius whimpered.

"He saw the storm." The unexpected, calm voice surprised the men. They whirled toward the sound and found Manx smiling at them. Darrius exhaled in relief while Stygian flashed his dagger.

Manx stood on the boulder with his arms folded across his chest. The devilish smile on his lips contrasted with the shadow of consternation in his eyes. He didn't appreciate Stygian torturing Darrius. There was no place in this world for cruelty. Manx tensed, releasing a subtle burst of energy. Darrius detected the blast of magic and prepared himself for what was to come.

"Explain yourself!" Stygian demanded, cautiously approaching the boulder, the battle dagger poised to strike.

Manx tilted his head. A corner of his mouth jerked up into an impish grin. "Explain myself?"

"First the tornado and now this vicious storm. Are you the perpetrator of these anomalies?"

"Anomalies?" Manx delighted playing this game with Stygian. But it was like poking a badger with his finger—eventually, someone would get hurt.

The Cererian's anger simmered near boiling and Darrius knew it would soon explode. He mentally messaged, *Manx, watch your tone with Stygian. He is very dangerous when vexed.*

Manx discreetly winked at Darrius and replied, *The frantic bird will settle down once his wings are clipped.* Darrius frowned. Manx's riddle made no sense. Anxiety gnawed at his stomach, but he trusted his friend.

"Do you mock me, magician?" Stygian menaced Manx with the dagger.

Manx snapped his finger and vanished, reappearing behind Stygian. "I do not mock you Stygian."

Stygian whirled, thrusting his dagger forward. But Manx had already disappeared leaving wispy smoke in his place. Abruptly, the magician reappeared behind Stygian again.

"If you'll settle down, I'll explain."

"Vile creature!" Enraged, Stygian stabbed at Manx. But the magician vanished again.

Darrius tensed. He sensed Stygian's rage. Like a roiling pot of stew, his lid would soon blow if Darrius didn't defuse the situation. Manx could clearly take care of himself, but Darrius worried for the soldiers who would not be able to defend themselves against their enraged commander. He sucked in a deep, cleansing breath, hoping to calm his nerves before placing a gentle hand on Stygian's shoulder. "Stygian, he is proving a point."

Manx reappeared on the boulder. Stygian glared at him while hissing at Darrius, "And what point is that Darrius? To make me implode?"

"My point, dear Stygian is that you are not asking the correct questions." Manx's eyes twinkled. "All that you've experienced are natural occurrences. This is the genuine world in which you exist. So, when you asked about anomalies, I could not truthfully respond to that question since there were none. Do you understand?"

Stygian eyed Manx. He didn't trust the magical being who twisted his words and toyed with him as if he was a lowly creature, and not a powerful Cererian commander. He decided to probe for more information and find out how this magician was able to travel in the manner that he does. "Everything is natural?"

"Yes, what you see is what you get."

"Then, how are you able to vanish and reappear?"

Manx smirked. Stygian's question was tricky and not easy to answer.

Manx leapt from the boulder with his arms spread wide. His demeanor shifted from cautious young man to affable friend. A warm smile curled his mouth as he announced, "Denali can have a wondrous effect on anyone walking within her world. And there is great power to be mined within her energy field." He could tell Stygian was intrigued so he continued, "All of her creatures have extraordinary abilities, and no two are alike."

Stygian considered Manx's words before offering, "So, what you're saying is that I have unique powers as well?"

"Exactly! And your power is different from mine or Darrius's."

At this point, Darrius was befuddled. Was Manx evading Stygian's question, or was it true, that each person—every soldier in camp—had unique powers yet untapped? He studied Stygian who rubbed his chin and gazed at the ground. If Manx was purposely misleading Stygian, he cleverly delivered the lie in a pretty package only an arrogant Cererian would appreciate.

Satisfied with the answer, Stygian sheathed his dagger. "I agree. Since arriving, I've felt incredible changes occurring within my body. I sense new powers emerging."

Darrius messaged Manx, *Did you trance him? This is the first time I'm hearing this information.*

I did not hypnotize your friend. He speaks the truth for once. What you see before you is a man who thirsts for much more than what he possesses.

"My apologies for being brusque, Manx. But you are a puzzle to me. I guess the energy of this land has impacted all of us."

Manx nodded. "Yes, the land of Denali can have a wonderful effect on all living things, but she can also remove your gifts without warning." Stygian's eyes darkened as if Manx's words sucked the daylight from the land. He didn't appreciate being controlled by anyone, much less by an earth spirit he could not hear or see.

Manx suddenly cleared his throat, grabbing the Cererians' attention. "My original purpose for visiting today was to extend an invitation to visit our village."

Darrius's heart raced. Memories of their passionate embrace in Manx's home released a torrent of desire. Provocative images and lusty thoughts filled his mind. What was wrong with him? Cererians don't act this way. He wondered if the host, who contributed to his human form, behaved this way when he was alive. He sucked in a breath that caught in his throat, causing him to gag. Stygian noticed. "Are you okay?"

"I'm fine, Stygian. I feel, like you, that the energy has had a profound impact on me."

Manx noticed Darrius's struggles and grinned an evil smile. He messaged. *Don't worry, I won't try anything tonight. But...maybe later.*

Darrius gasped and immediately stared at the ground, cloaking his emotions.

Stygian turned to Manx. "We accept your invitation. Where shall we meet you and when?"

"Nightfall, and we shall come to you." Before Stygian could say anything else Manx disappeared. Darrius was relieved to see him go. Emotions still swirled in his body, and he wasn't sure what would've happened if Manx continued to stand before him. And he didn't want Stygian detecting anything abnormal.

"*They* will come to us? How is that possible?" Stygian was perplexed by the magician's comment.

"I guess *they* will arrive as Manx appears...suddenly." Darrius stifled a chuckle. Being spontaneous and silly were new to him, but he loved it. He felt like a child seeing the world for the first time, and he wanted to play in it a lot more; and he wanted Manx by his side.

Chapter 5

Midsummer Feast

THE SUN NEVER SETS in the Alaskan summer. Though it may kiss the horizon, the sun stands its ground refusing to yield against the full darkness of night. If the magician and his village were arriving at nightfall, exactly when would that moment occur?

Stygian ordered his soldiers to dress for a visit from the local tribe.

"Sir, since the sun doesn't set during this time of the year, exactly when she we expect our visitors?" Andee asked.

Stygian's eyes darkened in thought. *Manx had said nightfall, but if the sun never sets...*

"What foolishness is this?" Stygian directed at Darrius as if his friend could explain the magician's motives. "I tire of Manx's games." Exasperated, he turned toward Denali's distant mountain peak lost in thought. So many bizarre events had occurred since their arrival on Earth and every one of them could be traced back to the mountain or Manx. *There's a magical connection between the two and I intend to tap into that power,* he mused.

Darrius examined Stygian's blank face. Although he tried, it was harder to read his friend's mind as he had blocked all mental messages choosing instead to become more isolated and withdrawn. He behaved as if Darrius and the soldiers were annoyances to be ignored or pawns to perform his bidding. Thane and Everild didn't mind following their leader's orders without question, but Andee and Benedict had grown increasingly wary of his actions.

Darrius shrugged. "It's his way. Manx is spontaneous and fun-loving." Darrius omitted all the other details he knew about the magician. While it was definitely a trait of his carefree friend, Manx's blithe behavior was the exact opposite of the rigid Cererian manner. "Perhaps it's the way of this world."

Stygian snorted. "I don't like it. I can't control the situation if I don't know what to expect."

Andee added, "Commander, the knowledge acquired by the Harvesters indicates that gatherings are typically planned for early evening."

"Very well. We'll assemble by the boulder in three hours. Tell the others."

"Yes, Commander!" Andee rushed away to inform Benedict, Thane, and Everild.

Five o'clock arrived. Flanked by his soldiers, Stygian awaited Manx in his formal Cererian uniform—a dark blue jacket with gold buttons and matching pants with a thin, gold stripe running the length of the leg. Darrius and the soldiers wore all-black outfits—an intentional arrangement by Stygian so the visitors would know who was in charge.

Darrius cared little for Stygian's rationale. But if wearing the oppressive black uniform would placate his friend, he would gladly put it on. His friend's human body sweated profusely bound up in the tight clothing. His constant panting belied how much Stygian suffered while waiting for the magician.

Minutes crept by. Stygian fidgeted, yanking at his collar, and swiping the torrents of sweat from his face with the back of his hand. He anxiously glanced to Darrius before peering at the sun that hovered on the horizon expecting it to move aside for the black of night that would never come.

Thirty minutes passed. "Where is that magician?" Stygian growled, a sneer snaking across his face. "This is not how you treat a Commander!" Darrius sighed. As much as he loved Manx's spontaneous side, his unpredictable behavior created animosity.

Sixty minutes. The soldiers awaited Manx at the boulder. Stygian's jacket was on the ground. His white undershirt was soaked through with sweat. The soldiers were forbidden to remove theirs and remained at attention swaying with the lazy heat that swirled around them. Darrius had already removed his jacket and carefully draped it over the limb of a nearby tree. The red sun hung just above the horizon, lingering on the lip of the Earth. Stygian glared at the orb and seethed, "I tire of this natural world. I tire of this magician who likes to play games." He turned toward his soldiers and ordered, "Back to camp. Now!"

The Cererians had just reached the outskirts of their campsite when a stiff breeze pushed through their ranks cooling their skin and kicking gravel against their boots. Benedict noticed the tent fabric flapping furiously and searched the sky for an approaching storm but found something much more astounding as he gazed back toward the boulder. He tapped his father on the shoulder. He tried to speak, but the words wouldn't form on his lips. All he could do was point and grunt. When Andee followed his son's gesture, his eyes widened as he squeaked in a hoarse whisper, "They're here."

Thane and Everild whirled following their comrade's gaze. The unexpected spectacle stunned them into silence as they gawked at hundreds of people spread across the space once occupied by the deep-water lake. The villagers busied themselves preparing meals and building tables for a feast. Standing front and center was Manx dressed in white. And, though the breeze still gusted, his clothes did not flutter. He saw the soldiers notice him and bowed in their direction.

Thane tapped Darrius on the shoulder and pointed toward the village before rushing away to alert Stygian. Darrius found Manx looking right at him. The two men shared a warm smile. A psychic pull lured Darrius to join the magician as though Manx had lightly tugged on a slim thread linking their hearts. Darrius quickened his pace to the village anxious to be with Manx again.

Frustrated and brooding, Stygian had left the camp. He stared off into the distance. Thane cautiously approached, fearful of disturbing his leader. "Commander, the village has appeared, and so has the magician, Manx."

Stygian slowly turned, his face a mixture of rage and agitation, his hands clenched into fists. Thane impulsively backed up. "My apologies for delivering disturbing news, Commander." Thane lowered his head, hoping his submissiveness would quell Stygian's urge to beat him.

Stygian relaxed his hands. "Where are the others?"

"Darrius has already joined the magician. But the soldiers await your command." Thane bowed his head again.

"Darrius left without us?" Stygian mulled over his friend's action. They had arrived on Earth as a cohesive unit, a strong band of soldiers and now, a crack appeared. Darrius stepped outside the normal constraints for a Cererian. His actions were an affront to Stygian's leadership. He would personally deal with his brother later. "Well, we need to join him, don't we?" Stygian's response was out of character for the gruff Cererian. Thane averted his eyes as Stygian shoved him aside and marched back to camp. "Walk with me, Thane. Let's get the others and visit this mysterious village."

The Cererians approached the bustling community. Following the custom of their planet, they all bowed their heads to Manx as a sign of respect.

"How nice of you to finally arrive," Stygian remarked. His comment was laced with poison, but Manx disregarded the veiled hostility.

Manx politely returned their bow. "How wonderful that you and your men could join us for the feast. 'Tis the time of the Summer Solstice and festivities will soon begin. My people welcome you to the harvest. What is ours is yours." Manx beamed at the Cererian leader. But his mental message to Darrius was ominous,

Your Cererian brother has evil in his heart. Things are not as they appear. A storm brews in your friend and the fury will soon be released.

Shocked by Manx's comment, Darrius wanted to reach out to his friend, but Stygian swiftly sidled up to him, "What a surprise, Darrius, to find you here. Did you not want to join your Cererian brothers in our formal welcoming party?"

Darrius searched Stygian's eyes. The pupils had enlarged, creating two black holes ringed with a halo of emerald-green—a predator's stare.

Stygian, your comment is unwarranted. You may have assumed leadership, but when we arrived on Earth, we arrived as equals. You are my brother, and I respect the memories we share, but in this world, you do not rule me.

Moments passed—awkward tense minutes—as the two men stared at each other assessing each other's intentions. Abruptly, Stygian spoke, responding to the magician, "Thank you for your hospitality, Manx. We look forward to learning more about you and your people." The Cererian surveyed the community—hundreds of people stoked fires and prepared the feast while others toiled on a large wooden structure. "How is this possible, Manx? How did you arrive without our knowledge?"

"This land runs deep with magical energy that flows directly from Mount Denali. This mystical force allows us to do wondrous things. Come with me, and I'll explain further about our community." Manx motioned for the Cererians to follow him, which they gladly did, eagerly drinking in the unusual sights and keenly listening to Manx's words. Under the cover of curiosity, Stygian accompanied the magician, feigning interest in his stories.

He brooded over Manx's reply, which avoided answering exactly how the village magically appeared. The magician was clever. Stygian yearned for Manx's power, but how would he gain access to those secrets?

As Manx led the group through the village, he chanced a look over his shoulder, hoping to catch a glimpse of Darrius who maintained a respectful distance. Their eyes briefly locked. Manx's eyes flashed, propelling a dart of intense heat into Darrius's bloodstream. Passion's fire flared deep inside.

Darrius caught his breath and messaged, *Manx, stop that. Not here!*

Manx chuckled—a vibrant warble that sounded much like a tinkling bell.

"Merry midsummer!" an old woman hailed. She sat on a straw mat and bound sheaves of grasses together while humming a melodic tune. Her light blue eyes sparkled as she watched the strangers pass by.

"The same to you," Stygian greeted as he dipped his head in her direction. He discreetly leaned toward Andee and whispered, "What is midsummer?"

Andee consulted the database. "A celebration of the summer season usually held on the Summer Solstice."

Stygian studied Andee for a few moments and then turned away muttering, "Clear as mud."

Manx led them to a wooden structure. Men and women labored around the ten-foot-high framework of poles and wooden planks lashed together with braided vines.

"Today is a special day. Not only do we celebrate midsummer, but we honor our fallen warrior, Tobias." Manx gestured toward the workers behind him. "These men and women are relatives of this remarkable man who lived in this world for ninety years. Tonight, they will sing songs of his accomplishments and then set his pyre ablaze so his soul can reach the heavens and take his seat at his ancestral table."

"By the size of this structure, this man was of huge importance," Stygian observed.

Manx regarded the Cererian with kind eyes. "Everyone in this community is of huge importance. Later, you'll be able to witness the joy felt by all when we release our brother into the ether."

Manx paused. He gazed at the ground lost in the fond memories he shared with the fallen warrior. Manx was only eight years old when Tobias rescued him from a frozen tomb on Denali's slopes. The earth spirit had lured Manx into her icy kingdom during a dark winter night. His brilliant energy thrummed with intense power, and Denali knew it was time for the Chronicle to be born.

The sacred words would be scribed upon his body, and he would rule over the world's peaceful and magical realms. But he was not the only one tested that night. Tobias, an emerging warrior of great strength and fortitude, would prove himself worthy to be Denali's white knight—a chosen individual who would protect the Chronicle at all costs.

Unable to resist the Great Mother's bewitching call, Tobias armed himself and scaled the great mountain. Denali's only words to him were, *You must find the Chronicle, or you both perish on my slopes.*

Abruptly, Manx raised his head, a wide smile bowing across his face, "Come join me at the feast. I imagine you're all famished." He guided them to an area full of long wooden tables. Savory and sweet aromas lingered. "We prepared many delights including loaves of bread, roasted vegetables, and various meats. Grab a dish and make your selections. I reserved a table over there so we can talk." Manx pointed to a heavy oak table just a few yards away and quickly departed.

The smell of fresh meat ignited a deep hunger within Stygian. Since their arrival on Earth, the soldiers had consumed only Cererian rations and plants deemed safe for consumption. As though he hadn't eaten in years, Stygian piled slabs of four different types of meat onto his plate and ladled a brown juice smelling of herbs over the pile. He grabbed another plate and heaped vegetables of all different colors into the middle before adding two slices of fresh bread across the top.

"You have a healthy appetite," Manx observed, smiling politely as Stygian sat opposite him.

Stygian grunted, his eyes riveted on the food. Wooden utensils had carefully been placed at each setting, but Stygian opted to use his hands. Hunched over his plate, he plunged his fingers into the meat scooping handfuls into his mouth. Gravy smeared both cheeks and trickled down his chin. He snatched a slice of bread and wiped his face before shoving it into his mouth. After several mouthfuls, he finally glanced up. Satisfaction filled his face as he chewed loudly, smacking his lips.

Manx winced. Stygian's barbaric display was truly offensive and not characteristic of a commander. He pondered why a man of rigid decorum would suddenly behave like an uncivilized boor. He messaged Darrius, *Is this how your friend typically acts at formal gatherings?*

Darrius sat beside Manx observing Stygian's feeding frenzy with dismay. This was not Cererian behavior at all. They grew up understanding the nuances of proper etiquette. *This is not the man I know. First, his unexpected rage escalated, and now this callous behavior has emerged. Is this the effect of Denali's energy on his body?*

Manx watched Stygian shove another hunk of meat into his mouth and pull the fat off with his teeth. *I think this is the effect of his host body. Your scientists said you would adopt the emotional and physical traits of the donor. Who was Stygian's host?*

The Harvesters assumed he was a Nordic warrior based on the age of his tomb and the remnants of a nearby village. What they didn't know was why his grave was devoid of any funerary tributes and had been placed far away from the village gates.

Interesting. Many tribes in the northern countries celebrate their warriors with funeral pyres, allowing their spirits to ascend to the afterlife. What if he was buried away from the village because they didn't want him in their midst? What if, this warrior was so evil, that his people punished him with eternal banishment?

The possibility intrigued Darrius. The Harvesters collected vast amounts of information on his own host body because of available written records, but the corpse supplying the DNA for Stygian was far too ancient for there to be any available data. Assumptions were made about his origins and his life in general.

Unlike their leader, Thane, Everild, Andee, and Benedict bowed their heads in reverence and asked for blessings for their meal. Then they noticed Stygian shoving his face into a plate of meat like a bear ripping into a salmon's flopping body. Puzzled by his actions, they hesitated. Darrius noticed their confusion and nodded toward their plates—a sign to continue eating as they were taught. The soldiers nodded back and ate their meals in silence.

Stygian turned his head to one side and belched a sickening roar before shoveling another scoop of food into his mouth. Some villagers who had joined them in friendship, politely left, casting worried glances toward the Cererian leader. Darrius watched them leave and sighed. It hurt to see the disgust clouding their faces. He couldn't take any more of Stygian's rude behavior and mentally messaged, *Brother, a little decorum, please. We are guests here. We are Cererians.*

With his elbows planted on the table, Stygian gnawed a huge turkey leg. Darrius's message drifted through his brain and he stopped mid-chew. Skin remnants dangled from his lip as he slowly faced Darrius. Without warning, Stygian slapped his friend across the face. A handprint of grease and meat blemished his smooth cheek. Manx gasped. The soldiers stopped eating and stared.

Stygian warned, *What I do is my own business, brother. Remember your place.*

Shocked and disappointed by Stygian's cruel attack, Darrius drew in several long, calming breaths. Despite his brother's brutish behavior, Darrius would not retaliate. Instead, his intuition urged him to seek serene and peaceful measures. He casually glanced at

Manx whose eyes were still wide in disbelief. He raised his napkin and dabbed his cheek, removing all the greasy remains. Then he ceremoniously folded it and placed it neatly on the table.

Calmly he stood and announced, "Thank you, Manx, for your invitation and for your wonderful food, but I must depart and return to camp."

As he lifted a leg over the bench, Stygian clamped a hand around Darrius's thigh and growled, "You are going nowhere, Darrius." His tone was so menacing that the other soldiers cringed from the hostile energy that exploded over the table. "Sit down...now!"

"Release your hand, Stygian. Remember you are the Commander of our group. These people—our hosts—judge us based on your behavior, not ours." Darrius stood firm hoping his ingratiating use of "Commander" would placate his friend. Tense moments passed.

Manx saw a flicker of normality in Stygian's eyes, which softened as he pondered Darrius's words. The Cererian leader released his friend's leg. His eyes shifted back and forth as he mentally reviewed various scenarios in his mind.

"Yes, you are correct, Darrius." Stygian's tone took a dramatic turn, surprising everyone. Turning to Manx he offered an apology, "I meant no disrespect. I have not been myself lately. This cursed heat affects me in the most unusual ways."

Stygian's ruse did not deceive Darrius who messaged Manx, *Stygian is not remorseful. There is something he wants, and to get it he must appease you.*

Manx smiled politely at Stygian. "Your apology is graciously accepted." He quickly followed up with Darrius, *I am fully aware of his tricks. He yearns to know the secrets to my power and my community's magic. We will see what his next move might be.* Manx abruptly turned to Darrius and winked.

Stygian noticed the gesture and was just about to utter a comment when Manx announced, "The funeral pyre is being prepared. I would be honored if you and your soldiers would accompany me to the memorial service for Tobias. He was a deeply respected warrior and would have loved to have met our Cererian guests. It is an honor to hold the flame that begins the warrior's journey. Stygian, would you consent to light the pyre?"

Stygian swiped residual turkey fat from his lips with the back of his hand and sat back, studying his host.

Manx was clever indeed. Stroking Stygian's ego was the perfect tactic for keeping the Cererian close. A peaceful calm washed over his face. His emerald-green eyes sparkled. For a brief moment, Darrius recognized his old friend, his kind and compassionate brother. "I would be greatly honored to do this for you," Stygian declared. "Very proud indeed."

Chapter 6

The Funeral Pyre

THE RECTANGULAR FUNERAL PYRE reached ten feet into the sky and stretched twenty feet long and perfectly aligned to the north. Seasoned oak poles and planks formed the skeleton of the massive framework. Willow branches wove throughout the structure while braided vines strapped everything together forming a strong and sturdy construction. A bier built on the very top awaited Tobias's body.

Fresh tree branches representing the natural elements were fastened onto each corner: oak was placed in the north to represent earth, a fragrant cedar branch was placed in the east to represent air, a colorful holly limb was affixed to the south to represent fire, and an elm branch was tied to the western corner to represent water. Fresh flowers and herbs were then woven throughout the structure. Lupines, fireweed, sage, and forget-me-nots decorated every tier while their sweet scents swirled among the assembled villagers.

Individuals formed a loose circle around the structure. Children sat in the front while adults stood behind them. Excitement charged the air as people shared stories about Tobias and repeated many of his bawdy jokes. Despite the somber event, this was an occasion for celebration, a time for renewal. Death shouldn't be feared. It was merely another stage in the soul's journey to the afterlife, and the joy found in the stars above.

A soft, calm melody drifted into the gathering and the chatter stopped. All eyes turned toward the opening in the circle. A trio of musicians—a fiddler, a flutist, and a drummer—solemnly entered playing a mournful tune. They led a procession of relatives who carried their patriarch on a wooden litter. The drummer thumped his hand drum slow and steady like a heartbeat while four generations of family members filed into the sacred space.

Tobias's grandsons lowered the litter to the ground.

A black bear hide enshrouded the warrior. His fighting dagger was tucked near his chest under the vine securing the hide against his body. His hunting spear lay beside him on one side while his bow constructed of maple, lay on the other side along with his deerskin quiver and arrows. Tobias's wife, Elena, knelt beside the litter gently touching her husband's head. At the age of ninety-eight, she was not strong enough to carry her husband to the pyre, as was their custom, but she would not leave her beloved's side until his moment of freedom drew near.

Manx entered the circle reciting the warrior's prayer. The Cererians didn't recognize the language, which was a mixture of musical sounds and syllables strewn together in a melodic song. As he sang, he approached each family member and bowed. When he reached Elena he embraced her, hugging her thin frame while tears flowed from their eyes. Tobias had saved his life. The moment he found Manx on Denali's snowy slope an unbreakable bond was forged. A connection that could not be broken even though Tobias had departed this physical world. Manx quietly pulled away, gently brushing the tears from Elena's cheek before kissing her forehead.

The moment had arrived to lift Tobias atop the structure.

Two ladders, constructed of oak poles, were steadied against the side of the frame. Two of the strongest grandsons knelt by the litter and hoisted Tobias. As family members gathered below, the two men ascended the ladders one slow step at a time. Each man climbed with one hand while gripping the litter in the other—a tortuous process, but one they lovingly endured. At the top, they carried their grandfather to the bier, carefully lowered the litter, and secured it with thick vines. Then the grandsons gently uncovered the bearskin from his face so Tobias would be able to see the stars and find his way to the afterlife. They were not surprised to see a plump, fresh face with vivid blue eyes staring back at them. This was the way of their magical world, and they accepted it as the ultimate truth.

After bowing respectively to their patriarch, the men climbed back down and removed the ladders. Manx ushered the relatives to assemble around the pyre and face their friends. One by one, young and old, each person sang the accomplishments of Tobias. Twenty emotional voices related the achievements and deeds of a strong warrior and beloved man.

Stygian squirmed with impatience. After two hours of procession and songs, he grew anxious to light the wood ablaze. There was something about destruction and the burning of a body that appealed to him. Memories poked at him, remembrances that weren't his. He saw himself in a foreign world—a cold, harsh climate with monstrous animals and massive sheets of ice. Stygian saw himself as a warrior, his body covered in the skins of the animals he vanquished, and his belt adorned with the teeth of individuals he had killed. He walked the world alone, banished from his settlement years earlier for killing the leader of the tribe and defiling his daughter.

Stygian choked on the bile rising in his throat. He was Cererian. He had never lived in that world. He had never performed the deeds he just witnessed. Yet, as he watched Tobias being placed lovingly atop the wooden structure, he yearned to be him. It was an unsatisfied longing to be remembered by loved ones and to embark on a warrior's journey into the heavens. These feelings were unusual to him. They were not his memories, yet somehow these blurred images were merging with his reality. They were snippets of another time in another body. He could see clearly through the other man's eyes and felt his disappointment and rage.

A three-year-old girl was the last to sing. Elena held the shy youngster in her arms gently urging her to express her love for the old warrior she knew as Baba. The little girl related a tale of the mighty warrior rescuing her from a tiny bunny in the garden. Sobs and chuckles peppered the gathering. It was the perfect ending to a somber declaration. Manx playfully winked at the little girl as Elena carried her from the circle.

Manx motioned for Stygian to join him by the fire. Nearby, a villager attended a small bonfire—a sacred blaze used only for hallowed ceremonies. Charred logs from previous burns are used in igniting a new fire—a method employed for generations to ensure that spiritual magic is reignited each time. The Cererian rose and straightened his uniform, carefully peering around the crowd to ensure all eyes were on him. He walked slowly to Manx. This was his moment to impress the villagers with his swagger and his confidence. Manx observed his display with an arched eyebrow and messaged Darrius, *The peacock struts. Ego has no place in this world.*

Darrius cupped his hand over his mouth, suppressing a chuckle.

Manx forced a smile at the Cererian who finally joined him. Turning to the crowd, Manx cleared his throat and announced, "Today is a special day as we honor our fallen warrior, Tobias. There is not a soul here who has not been impacted by his kindness, his deeds, or his bawdy stories. Tobias once told me that if he were to die, he hoped it would be at the hands of a rollicking good joke. Alas, that was not to be. But, tonight, we will drink and tell his stories. I only hope we recount his tales with justice. My friend, my trusted confidant, I will truly miss our times together on the slopes of Denali."

Stygian's ears perked up. Tobias and Manx spent time together on Denali. Perhaps this dead villager had had powers just like

Manx. The muscles bunched in Stygian's jaws as he mulled over the possibilities.

"And now, I'm honored to introduce a guest who hails from a faraway place, Ceres. He will do us the honor of lighting the pyre. Stygian, do you accept the flame of immortality?" Manx asked.

Transfixed by the pageantry and the formal announcement of his name, Stygian stood a little taller, his chin jutted out, and a smirk spread across his face. An overwhelming sense of pride swept over him. Hearing his name spoken aloud was familiar, but there was an undertone of peculiarity as though his name was uttered in the wrong language. Abruptly, a vision stabbed into his brain. He was looking through the eyes of the stranger who recently assaulted him with memories from another world. A large man towered over him tapping a sword on both of his shoulders and proclaiming his name to the tribe. Stygian shook his head hoping to scatter the foreign images.

"Stygian? Do you accept the flame?" Manx's voice penetrated the thickness of the vision pulling Stygian back to reality.

The Cererian smiled broadly, hoping the villagers didn't notice anything amiss, and replied, "Yes, I accept the flame of immortality."

Manx placed a large torch into Stygian's hand. The gnarled bunch of thick braided limbs interwoven with willow branches extended almost four feet in length. "Please ignite the torch from the sacred blaze and carry it to the pyre."

Stygian plunged it into the bonfire and the torch quickly ignited, showering the dusky night sky with yellow sparks like fireflies drifting to the heavens. He stared at the firebrand as he twirled it in his hands transfixed on the yellow flames licking and snapping through the twists of willow and oak.

"Follow me, Stygian." Manx gestured toward a dangling cloth hanging near one pole. The red and white fabric—remnants of Tobias's blanket—snaked up the pole and led directly to the bier of sticks supporting Tobias's body.

Stygian gazed up the pyre and tears welled as a deep melancholy filled his heart. He shook his head, annoyed at his emotional display. But he *was* sad. Not for Tobias but for himself and the warrior's funeral he never received.

What nonsense is this?

Stygian felt like a man torn in half—on one side stood a confident Cererian commander and on the other lurked a disgruntled warrior seeking retribution from beyond the grave.

"Stygian?" Manx's gentle words couldn't penetrate the Cererian's mind as he struggled between the two worlds. Manx repeated himself, a little louder, "Stygian, you can light the pyre."

"Yes." Stygian slowly blinked as he returned to this world, leaving the ice glaciers on the other side. "Yes, Manx. I am ready to proceed." Without ceremony he stepped forward and lit the bottom edge of the cloth. The flame fled quickly up the blanket licking the wooden poles, dried vines and planks along the way. When the bright blaze reached Tobias it torched the kindling placed inside his bier and erupted in a golden explosion. Fire sparks shot into the sky like newborn stars seeking to take their place in the heavens above.

Darrius took the torch from Stygian and threw it into the sacred blaze and then guided him to the safety of the outer circle where they could safely watch the burning. "It's so beautiful..." Stygian's voice trailed off.

Manx searched Stygian's face. Tears pooled and a trickle flowed down the bridge of his nose. He reached out to Darrius, *Stygian is crying. This is very unexpected.*

Crying? I've never seen him cry.

"Manx?" Stygian's unexpected question surprised the magician.

"Yes, Stygian."

"What are those wisps of smoke?" Stygian pointed to a cloud of luminescent tendrils huddled around the burning remains of the bier.

"What you are witnessing is Tobias's lifeforce reaching for the heavens. Is it not magical?"

Stygian snapped his head toward Manx. "Did Tobias have special gifts?"

Manx studied Stygian. He was aware of his motives and understood his line of questioning. "He had many talents. As I mentioned earlier, this land is the core of our existence and we all feed from its energy."

An explosion from above surprised the spectators and they instinctively stepped back. The solid platform under the bier had burned too quickly and collapsed, crashing down through the middle of the structure. The crowd scattered as embers and burning branches rained down on them. Stygian watched the destruction with glee. The raging fire tantalized him, and excited him. Then he saw it, the wispy fingers of smoke burrowing out of the middle of the wooden structure, searching for the sky, seeking the heavens. Stygian drew near to see them closer.

Manx laid a gentle hand on his shoulder to pull him back, but Stygian whipped his head around and snarled, "How dare you touch me, magician!" Stygian yanked free and crept closer to the perimeter, the inferno scorching his face. The smoky fingers curled in front of him, probing the air and seeking the ether. But Stygian saw it as an enticement, an invitation. "Oh yes," he whispered, "I want to go with you."

Manx followed the Cererian. "Stygian, please don't go any further. I implore you!"

Stygian glared at Manx with solid black eyes, an evil grin slicing his face. In that moment Manx knew Stygian had yielded to the evil within. The Cererian returned to the fire and the tempting wisps wriggling through the wreckage, seeking freedom.

He pushed a hand out toward them. "Come here, I won't hurt you."

"No, don't touch them!" Manx screamed.

Surprised by the magician's cry Stygian gulped a breath inadvertently sucking in the smoky tendrils.

He fell to the ground wheezing and clawing at his throat.

Manx frantically searched the air for Tobias's lifeforce, but it was gone, consumed by the Cererian. *Darrius, he has swallowed the life essence of my friend, Tobias. Your evil friend has stolen his soul and his magic!*

Darrius knelt beside Manx. *What can we do? How can we extract the essence? Through coughing? Through vomiting?* Manx shook his head as he and Darrius held Stygian to the ground. The Cererian thrashed in agony, clawing at his throat and gulping for air. His eyes bulged out of their sockets while trickles of blood streamed from the corners. Tobias's spirit was locked within the fleshy walls of his human prison. Despite its efforts, the lifeforce could not escape. Stygian suddenly grew still, collapsing into the arms of unconsciousness.

"I'm sure Andee can determine how to make this right." Darrius offered this as hope, even though he sensed nothing could be done.

Manx lightly touched Darrius's cheek and peered into his eyes. Sorrow reddened his eyes. *My dear Darrius. The storm is upon us. This is the beginning of the end.*

Chapter 7

Darkness Descends

"Andee, there must be a way to release Tobias's soul. Try harder!" The elderly soldier eyed Darrius. His friend's anguished behavior was unsettling. Darrius was always the calm voice, the composed Cererian who could de-escalate Stygian's wild temper and restore peace to the camp. Now, Darrius paced beside the commander's body, his hands running through his hair, his face twisted in desperation. "Andee, please!"

Andee's heart ached for Darrius, but he felt no pity for his commander lying in front of him, his fingers rigid and bent like claws; his eyes rolled back as foam dribbled out of his mouth. "I have searched, Darrius, but there is no precedent for what has occurred. I fear there is no help for Stygian."

"That's not good enough!" Darrius teetered on the verge of panic. The earth spirit was right. Evil had accompanied him to Earth and that menace was Stygian. He witnessed the beast gradually claim his friend, but he was always able to call him back from the edge. He had realized he betrayed both Manx and Stygian. Standing by, helpless, as they both experienced their torments, all because he didn't stop the beast.

Manx wrapped his arm around Darrius and pulled him close. Even in his own moment of sorrow, his friend's anguish was more upsetting. "You have not betrayed me, Darrius."

Darrius searched Manx's eyes. "If I had prevented him from attending the festival, Tobias would be well on his way to the heavens, and Stygian wouldn't be dying."

"Nothing would have prevented this outcome. I have known for some time that this day would come."

Darrius frowned. "What do you mean you've known for some time?"

A smile crept across Manx's face. "My dear Darrius, Mother Denali has always known. She foretold the unfortunate events. Stygian would interfere with Tobias's passage regardless of what you and I did." He gently kissed Darrius on the forehead. "There is a way to save Tobias's soul."

"There is? How? Whatever it is, let me know so I can right this wrong."

Manx sighed. His eyes darkened with sorrow. "For my friend's spirit to escape, Stygian must die. Only upon his death will Tobias be released into the ether."

Darrius shuddered. He couldn't kill his friend. It was against Cererian law to kill another.

Manx cautioned, "If he is not dispatched while he is vulnerable, while he is unconscious, the world will pay the price." He leaned close. His lips brushed Darrius's ear as he whispered, "Death is the only solution. If you or your men won't kill him, I will. When your friend inhaled Tobias's essence, a transformation began. Tobias was not just a great warrior, he was a powerful magician, and now his magic swirls inside Stygian just like the host DNA has impacted your abilities, so will Stygian be able to use Tobias's magic. And we know he won't use those talents to benefit the world."

"What do you mean the world will pay the price? What else did Denali share with you?"

Manx stroked Darrius's cheek with the back of his finger. "There is so much I wish I could share with you. But I cannot. I am bound by Denali. She alone can alter events, and I cannot interfere. Darrius, our time together grows short. Do what you must, what you know must be done to save our world...and your world." Manx snapped his fingers and vanished.

Swaddled in blankets, Stygian shivered violently. Guttural groans escaped between his ragged breaths. His host body wrestled with the spirit of the great warrior—their life forces locked in combat. Evil and good struggled for control of Stygian.

Darrius watched his friend writhe and whimper.

Manx's words flashed in his mind, *Death is the only solution.*

Darrius unsheathed his battle dagger and held it aloft. Light glinted off the blade's mirrored surface and the tips of the treacherous angled spikes. He glanced at his helpless friend. One plunge of the dagger would kill the Cererian. Using it now would relieve Stygian from his torment and would save the world. But just as the evil host's DNA consumed Stygian's body, the shaman who had contributed to Darrius urged him toward peaceful measures. Killing was not in his genetic makeup. Cererian logic pushed him to stab his friend and correct the misdeeds, but he couldn't. He wouldn't. Darrius hung his head in defeat. He would let nature's spirits decide if Stygian should die.

Darkness descends. The words fell through his mind like a leaf fluttering to the ground.

Twelve hours had passed.

Darrius had fallen asleep huddled into a ball, his knees drawn up to his chest while maintaining a vigil over his Cererian brother.

"Darrius?" The soft voice teased his sleep. "Darrius, wake up."

"Hmm?" Darrius mumbled, half awake.

"Darrius, this is Andee. We have an issue. Stygian—"

"What? What's going on?" Andee never finished his statement. The mere mention of Stygian's name roused Darrius from his dreams. He reached beside himself expecting to find his friend. Instead, he grabbed the discarded blankets that had covered Stygian. Confused, he looked at Andee. "Where did you take him?"

"Darrius. I...we did not move the commander. He ran from camp several hours ago."

Darrius rubbed his eyes. It was then that he saw the blood and dark purple bruises around Andee's head. "Andee, what happened to you?" Andee gazed to the ground avoiding Darrius's eyes. Darrius sensed a deep shame emanating from the old man. He rose and gently lifted Andee's chin.

Tears welled in his eyes as Andee choked, "He's gone. Benedict and I tried to hold him. But he's so strong." Andee sucked in a breath before continuing, "He turned on us, Darrius. He beat Benedict until he was unconscious and then threw me toward the boulder."

"Threw you? That boulder is over one hundred yards away."

"I know that sounds crazy, but he picked me up and tossed me as though I weighed nothing."

Darrius ran his fingers through his hair. Nothing made sense. "What about Thane and Everild?"

Andee shook his head. "They left with Stygian. He offered them great wealth and power, and they eagerly agreed to go." Andee held his head, sobbing, "I'm so sorry, Darrius. Benedict and I tried our best."

"Let's go to your son. Together we can heal his injuries." Darrius attempted to lead Andee away, but the old man stopped him.

"No, Darrius. I can heal my son. You need to stop Stygian. He ran toward the lake screaming he could see the village. I only saw water, but I think Tobias's spirit possessed some sort of magic, and Stygian has that power now." Andee gripped Darrius's arms and squeezed. The old man's strength surprised Darrius. "You need to stop him, Darrius. Go. Now!"

Darrius stood at the water's edge and surveyed the lake. He saw and felt nothing. The silence unnerved him, and he frantically reached out to Manx.

Manx are you here? Stygian escaped and I think he means you harm.

"I'm here, dear Darrius."

"Manx!" Darrius ran into his open arms and hugged him hard, not wanting to let him go. He looked up into his eyes, which were pale and weary. "Manx?"

"Darrius. You must leave. Stygian will kill you as well if you remain."

"Kill me as well? What do you mean?"

Manx glanced wistfully over the lake. "Even now, your friend kills my people and feeds upon their magic. Stygian has allowed Everild and Thane to feed upon the magicians' spirits. Now, they too, hunt and murder the villagers. Manx sank against Darrius. He searched Darrius's face with white, sightless orbs. "There isn't much time, dear friend."

"Manx, what's wrong? Why can't you fight them?"

Manx managed a weak smile. "My dear Darrius. I am fighting them. I am this land. I am the air. I am the people. But I weaken with each assault." Manx's body shuddered before flickering in and out like a fading photograph. Eventually, only a transparent image remained of the man Darrius loved.

Darrius's eyes widened. "Manx, what's happening?"

"Remember when we were first met, and you sensed I was a wispy image like a spirit?" A broad smile graced his face popping the familiar dimples. "That's exactly what I am. I am the essence of Denali's world. I am the Chronicle of this planet. For a millennium, Chronicles have maintained the peace and balance on Earth. The holy words are written on my body and once I am gone this land will be plunged into darkness. Sorrow and death will rule the world.

"No, this can't be happening. I don't want to lose you!" Darrius attempted to hug the magician, but his hands pushed through his ghostly frame.

"Darrius, listen carefully. We cannot undo the past, but we can plan for the future. In one thousand years, a new Chronicle will emerge to lead the magicians of the world. You, and others like you, must be the observers. Protect the Chronicle and guide them to the throne so the world will know balance and peace once again.

Mother Denali will always be with you. You carry the blood of a powerful shaman in your veins. Gather the other shamans hiding all over this planet and plan for the ascension of the next Chronicle. For when Stygian and his soldiers are finally vanquished, the souls of all the magicians they killed will be released to find the serenity of the ether."

Manx's transparent form flickered, and he smiled gently at Darrius. "My time has come to leave my dear Darrius. I will always love you." The spirit bent close and kissed Darrius gently on his upturned mouth. Darrius lingered wanting the moment to last forever, but in a whisper, Manx was gone.

Darkness descends.

Thank You

Thank you for reading **Darkness Descends**, the prequel to **Chronicle of Ceres.**

If you enjoyed this book, please take a moment to write a review.

It's important for a book to have social proof, and I'd love your help sharing this series with others who embrace their magic.

Leave a review or star rating at your favorite book retailer

For new releases, giveaways, and fun info, subscribe to my newsletter by visiting www.cllavigne.com

Acknowledgements

A strong nod to those amazing readers who support me, the Kemps and the Cererians in our magical world! Without you, my fantastical world would not exist.

The backbone to my writing is my husband, Chris, who weathers my emotional storms, calms me, and urges me to finish my fantastical tales.

Wayne provided guidance for this novella, reading it with his critical eye and sharpened red pen.

What would I do without my editor, Brittany? Imagine my stories without your intervention.

About Author

Born in Alaska and raised in England, CL writes horror and fantasy that have supernatural overtones. Her stories feature real people and natural magic, all controlled by the spirits of nature and otherworldly beings.

Residing in the Sunshine State with her husband, four cats and six goldfish, CL incorporates elements of magic, mysticism and mythology into her writings. It's not unusual to encounter dragons, elemental spirits, glowing orbs, and even bigfoot as you follow her characters on their adventures.

Her current magical realism fantasy series is Chronicle of Ceres, which features 5 books. The fifth, Ascension of the Chronicle, will release March 2026.

Tales From the Crows, her first collection of horror stories was recently published.

Embrace your magic!

Find the magic and stay informed about special deals, giveaways, new releases and other great updates by subscribing to her **NEWSLETTER.**

Discover CL's magic:

www.cllavigne.com

www.facebook.com/CLLaVigneAuthor

www.instagram.com/cllavigneauthor/

Also By

Chronicle of Ceres Magical Realism Series
Beginning of Tomorrows, book 1
Denali Rising, book 2
Shasta Beckons, book 3
Bluestone Shadows, book 4
Ascension of the Chronicle, book 5

Tales From the Crows
Horror short story collection